MANIAC MAGEE

Other Books Available in Paperback by Jerry Spinelli:
Jason and Marceline
Space Station Seventh Grade
Who Put That Hair in My Toothbrush?
The Bathwater Gang

MANIAC MAGEE

A NOVEL BY

JERRY SPINELLI

ITTLE, BROWN AND COMPANY
ew York   Boston

Little, Brown and Company

Hachette Book Group
237 Park Avenue, New York, NY 10017
Visit our website at www.lb-teens.com

Little, Brown and Company is a division of Hachette Book Group, Inc.
The Little, Brown name and logo are trademarks of Hachette Book Group, Inc.

First Paperback Edition: November 1999

Library of Congress Cataloging-in-Publication Data

Spinelli, Jerry.
    Maniac Magee: a novel/by Jerry Spinelli. — 1st ed.
        p.   cm.
    Summary: After his parents die, Jeffrey Lionel Magee's life
becomes legendary, as he accomplishes athletic and other
feats which awe his contemporaries.

ISBN 978 0-316-80722-7 (hc) / ISBN 978-0-316-80906-1 (pb)
    1. Title   89-27144
PZ7.S75663Man 1990
[Fic] — dc20
HC: 30 29 28 27 26 25 24
PB: 20   19   18   17

COM-MO
Printed in the United States of America

For Ray and Jerry Lincoln

MANIAC MAGEE

Before the Story

*T*hey say Maniac Magee was born in a dump. They say his stomach was a cereal box and his heart a sofa spring.

They say he kept an eight-inch cockroach on a leash and that rats stood guard over him while he slept.

They say if you knew he was coming and you sprinkled salt on the ground and he ran over it, within two or three blocks he would be as slow as everybody else.

They say.

What's true, what's myth? It's hard to know.

Finsterwald's gone now, yet even today you'll never find a kid sitting on the steps where he once lived. The Little League field is still there, and the band shell. Cobble's Corner still stands at the corner of Hector and Birch, and if you ask the man behind the counter, he'll take the clump of string out of a drawer and let you see it.

Grade school girls in Two Mills still jump rope and chant:

> Ma-niac, Ma-niac
> He's so *cool*
> Ma-niac, Ma-niac
> Don't go to *school*
> Runs all *night*
> Runs all *right*
> Ma-niac, Ma-niac
> Kissed a *bull!*

And sometimes the girl holding one end of the rope is from the West side of Hector, and the girl on the other end is from the East side; and if you're looking for Maniac Magee's legacy, or monument, that's as good as any — even if it wasn't really a bull.

But that's okay, because the history of a kid is one part fact, two parts legend, and three parts snowball. And if you want to know what it was like back when Maniac Magee roamed these parts, well, just run your hand under your movie seat and be very, very careful not to let the facts get mixed up with the truth.

PART I

1

*M*aniac Magee was not born in a dump. He was born in a house, a pretty ordinary house, right across the river from here, in Bridgeport. And he had regular parents, a mother and a father.

But not for long.

One day his parents left him with a sitter and took the P & W high-speed trolley into the city. On the way back home, they were on board when the P & W had its famous crash, when the motorman was drunk and took the high trestle over the Schuylkill River at sixty miles an hour, and the whole kaboodle took a swan dive into the water.

And just like that, Maniac was an orphan. He was three years old.

Of course, to be accurate, he wasn't really Maniac then. He was Jeffrey. Jeffrey Lionel Magee.

Little Jeffrey was shipped off to his nearest relatives, Aunt Dot and Uncle Dan. They lived in Hollidaysburg, in the western part of Pennsylvania.

Aunt Dot and Uncle Dan hated each other, but because they were strict Catholics, they wouldn't get a divorce. Around the time Jeffrey arrived, they stopped talking to each other. Then they stopped sharing.

Pretty soon there were two of everything in the house. Two bathrooms. Two TVs. Two refrigerators. Two toasters. If it were possible, they would have had two Jeffreys. As it was, they split him up as best they could. For instance, he would eat dinner with Aunt Dot on Monday, with Uncle Dan on Tuesday, and so on.

Eight years of that.

Then came the night of the spring musicale at Jeffrey's school. He was in the chorus. There was only one show, and one auditorium, so Aunt Dot and Uncle Dan were forced to share at least that much. Aunt Dot sat on one side, Uncle Dan on the other.

Jeffrey probably started screaming from the start of the song, which was "Talk to the Animals," but nobody knew it because he was drowned out by all the other voices. Then the music ended, and Jeffrey went right on screaming, his face bright red by now, his neck bulging. The music director faced the singers, frozen with his arms still raised. In the audience faces began to change. There was a quick smatter of giggling by some people who figured the screaming kid was some part of the show, some funny animal maybe. Then the giggling stopped, and eyes started to shift and heads started to turn, because now everybody could see that this wasn't part of the show at all, that little Jeffrey Magee wasn't supposed to be up there on the risers, pointing to his aunt and uncle, bellowing out from the midst of the chorus: "Talk! Talk, will ya! Talk! Talk! Talk!"

No one knew it then, but it was the birth scream of a legend.

And that's when the running started. Three springy steps down from the risers — girls in pastel dresses screaming, the music director lunging — a leap from the stage, out the side door and into the starry, sweet, onion-grass-smelling night.

Never again to return to the house of two toasters. Never again to return to school.

2

Everybody knows that Maniac Magee (then Jeffrey) started out in Hollidaysburg and wound up in Two Mills. The question is: What took him so long? And what did he do along the way?

Sure, two hundred miles is a long way, especially on foot, but the year that it took him to cover it was about fifty-one weeks more than he needed — figuring the way he could run, even then.

The legend doesn't have the answer. That's why this period is known as The Lost Year.

And another question: Why did he stay here? Why Two Mills?

Of course, there's the obvious answer that sitting right across the Schuylkill is Bridgeport, where he was born. Yet there are other theories. Some say he just got tired of running. Some say it was the butterscotch Krimpets. And some say he only intended to pause here but that he stayed because he was so happy to make a friend.

If you listen to everybody who claims to have seen Jeffrey-Maniac Magee that first day, there must have been ten thousand people and a parade of fire trucks waiting for him at the town limits. Don't believe it. A couple of people truly remember, and here's what they saw: a scraggly little kid jogging toward them, the soles of both sneakers hanging by their hinges and flopping open like dog tongues each time they came up from the pavement.

But it was something they heard that made him stick in their minds all these years. As he passed them, he said, "Hi." Just that — "Hi" — and he was gone. They stopped, they blinked, they turned, they stared after him, they wondered: *Do I know that kid?* Because people just didn't say that to strangers, out of the blue.

3

*A*s for the first person to actually stop and talk with Maniac, that would be Amanda Beale. And it happened because of a mistake.

It was around eight in the morning, and Amanda was heading for grade school, like hundreds of other kids all over town. What made Amanda different was that she was carrying a suitcase, and that's what caught Maniac's eye. He figured she was like him, running away, so he stopped and said, "Hi."

Amanda was suspicious. Who was this white stranger kid? And what was he doing in the East End, where almost all the kids were black? And why was he saying that?

But Amanda Beale was also friendly. So she stopped and said "Hi" back.

"Are you running away?" Jeffrey asked her.

"Huh?" said Amanda.

Jeffrey pointed at the suitcase.

Amanda frowned, then thought, then laughed. She

laughed so hard she began to lose her balance, so she set the suitcase down and sat on it so she could laugh more safely. When at last she could speak, she said, "I'm not running away. I'm going to school."

She saw the puzzlement on his face. She got off the suitcase and opened it up right there on the sidewalk.

Jeffrey gasped. "Books!"

Books, all right. Both sides of the suitcase crammed with them. Dozens more than anyone would ever need for homework.

Jeffrey fell to his knees. He and Amanda and the suitcase were like a rock in a stream; the school-goers just flowed to the left and right around them. He turned his head this way and that to read the titles. He lifted the books on top to see the ones beneath. There were fiction books and nonfiction books, who-did-it books and let's-be-friends books and what-is-it books and how-to books and how-not-to books and just-regular-kid books. On the bottom was a single volume from an encyclopedia. It was the letter A.

"My library," Amanda Beale said proudly.

Somebody called, "Gonna be late for school, girl!"

Amanda looked up. The street was almost deserted. She slammed the suitcase shut and started hauling it along. Jeffrey took the suitcase from her. "I'll carry it for you."

Amanda's eyes shot wide. She hesitated; then she snatched it back. "Who *are* you?" she said.

"Jeffrey Magee."

"Where are you from? West End?"

"No."

She stared at him, at the flap-soled sneakers. Back in those days the town was pretty much divided. The East End was blacks, the West End was whites. "I know you're not from the East End."

"I'm from Bridgeport."

"Bridgeport? Over there? *That* Bridgeport?"

"Yep."

"Well, why aren't you there?"

"It's where I'm from, not where I am."

"Great. So where do you *live?*"

Jeffrey looked around. "I don't know . . . maybe . . . here?"

"*Maybe?*" Amanda shook her head and chuckled. "*May*be you better go ask your mother and father if you live here or not."

She speeded up. Jeffrey dropped back for a second, then caught up with her. "Why are you taking all these books to school?"

Amanda told him. She told him about her little brother and sister at home, who loved to crayon every piece of paper they could find, whether or not it already had type all over it. And about the dog, Bow Wow, who chewed everything he could get his teeth on. And that, she said, was why she carried her whole library to and from school every day.

First bell was ringing; the school was still a block away. Amanda ran. Jeffrey ran.

"Can I have a book?" he said.

"They're mine," she said.

"Just to read. To borrow."

"No."

"Please. What's your name?"

"Amanda."

"Please, Amanda. Any one. Your shortest one."

"I'm late now and I'm not gonna stop and open up this thing again. Forget it."

He stopped. "Amanda!"

She kept running, then stopped, turned, glared. What kind of kid was this, anyway? All grungy. Ripped shirt. Why didn't he go back to Bridgeport or the West End, where he belonged? Bother some white girl up there? And why was she still standing here?

"So what if I loaned you one, huh? How am I gonna get it back?"

"I'll bring it back. Honest! If it's the last thing I do. What's your address?"

"Seven twenty-eight Sycamore. But *you* can't come there. You can't even be *here*."

Second bell rang. Amanda screamed, whirled, ran.

"Amanda!"

She stopped, turned. "*Ohhhh,*" she squeaked. She tore a book from the suitcase, hurled it at him — "*Here!*" — and dashed into school.

The book came flapping like a wounded duck and fell at Jeffrey's feet. It was a story of the Children's Crusade. Jeffrey picked it up, and Amanda Beale was late to school for the only time in her life.

4

*J*effrey made three other appearances that first day.

The first came at one of the high school fields, during eleventh-grade gym class. Most of the students were playing soccer. But about a dozen were playing football, because they were on the varsity, and the gym teacher happened to be the football coach. The star quarterback, Brian Denehy, wound up and threw a sixty-yarder to his favorite receiver, James "Hands" Down, who was streaking a fly pattern down the sideline.

But the ball never quite reached Hands. Just as he was about to cradle it in his big brown loving mitts, it vanished. By the time he recovered from the shock, a little kid was weaving upfield through the varsity football players. Nobody laid a paw on him. When the kid got down to the soccer field, he turned and punted the ball. It sailed back over the up-looking gym-classers, spiraling more perfectly than anything

Brian Denehy had ever thrown, and landed in the outstretched hands of still stunned Hands Down. Then the kid ran off.

There was one other thing, something that all of them saw but no one believed until they compared notes after school that day: up until the punt, the kid had done everything with one hand. He had to, because in his other hand was a book.

5

*L*ater on that first day, there was a commotion in the West End. At 803 Oriole Street, to be exact. At the backyard of 803 Oriole, to be exacter.

This, of course, was the infamous address of Finsterwald. Kids stayed away from Finsterwald's the way old people stay away from Saturday afternoon matinees at a two-dollar movie. And what would happen to a kid who didn't stay away? That was a question best left unanswered. Suffice it to say that occasionally, even today, if some poor, raggedy, nicotine-stained wretch is seen shuffling through town, word will spread that this once was a bright, happy, normal child who had the misfortune of blundering onto Finsterwald's property.

That's why, if you valued your life, you never chased a ball into Finsterwald's backyard. Finsterwald's backyard was a graveyard of tennis balls and baseballs and footballs and Frisbees and model airplanes and one-way boomerangs.

That's why his front steps were the only un-sat-on front steps in town.

And why no paperkid would ever deliver there.

And why no kid on a snow day would ever shovel that sidewalk, not for a zillion dollars.

So, it was late afternoon, and screams were coming from Finsterwald's.

Who? What? Why?

The screamer was a boy whose name is lost to us, for after this day he disappears from the pages of history. We believe he was about ten years old. Let's call him Arnold Jones.

Arnold Jones was being hoisted in the air above Finsterwald's backyard fence. The hoisters were three or four high school kids. This was one of the things they did for fun. Arnold Jones had apparently forgotten one of the cardinal rules of survival in the West End: Never let yourself be near Finsterwald's and high school kids at the same time.

So, there's Arnold Jones, held up by all these hands, flopping and kicking and shrieking like some poor Aztec human sacrifice about to be tossed off a pyramid. "No! No! Please!" he pleads. "*Pleeeeeeeeeeeeese!*"

So of course, they do it. The high-schoolers dump him into the yard. And now they back off, no longer laughing, just watching, watching the back door of the house, the windows, the dark green shades.

As for Arnold Jones, he clams up the instant he hits the ground. He's on his knees now, all hunched and puckered. His eyes goggle at the back door, at the door knob. He's paralyzed, a mouse in front of the yawning maw of a python.

Now, after a minute or two of breathless silence, one of the high-schoolers thinks he hears something. He whispers: "Listen." Another one hears it. A faint, tiny noise. A rattling. A chittering. A chattering. And getting louder — yes — chattering teeth. Arnold Jones's teeth. They're chattering like snare drums. And now, as if his mouth isn't big enough to hold the chatter, the rest of his body joins in. First it's a buzz-like trembling, then the shakes, and finally it's as if every bone inside him is clamoring to get out. A high-schooler squawks: "He's got the finsterwallies!"*

"Yeah! Yeah!" they yell, and they stand there cheering and clapping.

Years later, the high-schoolers' accounts differ. One says the kid from nowhere hopped the fence, hopped it without ever laying a hand on it to boost himself over. Another says the kid just opened the back gate and strolled on in. Another swears it was a mirage, some sort of hallucination, possibly caused by evil emanations surrounding 803 Oriole Street.

Real or not, they all saw the same kid: not much bigger than Arnold Jones, raggedy, flap-soled sneakers, book in one hand. They saw him walk right up to Arnold, and they saw Arnold look up at him and

---

*fin·ster·wal·lies (fin′stĕr-wäl-ēz) *n*. [Two Mills, Pa., W. End] Violent trembling of the body, especially in the extremities (arms and legs)

faint dead away. Such a bad case of the finsterwallies did Arnold have that his body kept shaking for half a minute after he conked out.

The phantom Samaritan stuck the book between his teeth, crouched down, hoisted Arnold Jones's limp carcass over his shoulder, and hauled him out of there like a sack of flour. Unfortunately, he chose to put Arnold down at the one spot in town as bad as Finsterwald's backyard — namely, Finsterwald's front steps. When Arnold came to and discovered this, he took off like a horsefly from a swatter.

As the stupefied high-schoolers were leaving the scene, they looked back. They saw the kid, cool times ten, stretch out on the forbidden steps and open his book to read.

6

About an hour later Mrs. Valerie Pickwell twanged open her back screen door, stood on the step, and whistled.

As whistles go, Mrs. Pickwell's was one of the all-time greats. It reeled in every Pickwell kid for dinner every night. Never was a Pickwell kid *ever* late for dinner. It's a record that will probably stand forever. The whistle wasn't loud. It wasn't screechy. It was a simple two-note job — one high note, one low. To an outsider, it wouldn't sound all that special. But to the ears of a Pickwell kid, it was magic. Somehow it had the ability to slip through the slush of five o'clock noises to reach its targets.

So, from the dump, from the creek, from the tracks, from Red Hill — in ran the Pickwell kids for dinner, all ten of them. Add to that the parents, baby Didi, Grandmother and Grandfather Pickwell, Great-grandfather Pickwell, and a down-and-out taxi driver whom Mr. Pickwell was helping out (the Pickwells were always helping out somebody) — all that, and you had what Mrs. Pickwell called her "small nation."

Only a Ping-Pong table was big enough to seat them all, and that's what they ate around. Dinner was spaghetti. In fact, every third night dinner was spaghetti.

When dinner was over and they were all bringing their dirty dishes to the kitchen, Dominic Pickwell said to Duke Pickwell, "Who's that kid?"

"What kid?" said Duke.

"The kid next to you at the table."

"I don't know. I thought Donald knew him."

"I don't know him," said Donald. "I thought Dion knew him."

"Never saw him," said Dion. "I figured he was Deirdre's new boyfriend."

Deirdre kicked Dion in the shins. Duke checked back in the dining room. "He's gone!"

The Pickwell kids dashed out the back door to the top of Rako Hill. They scanned the railroad tracks. There he was, passing Red Hill, a book in his hand. He was running, passing the spear field now, and the Pickwell kids had to blink and squint and shade their eyes to make sure they were seeing right — because the kid wasn't running the cinders alongside the tracks, or the wooden ties. No, he was running — *running* — where the Pickwells themselves, where every other kid, had only ever walked — on the steel rail itself!

7

When Jeffrey Magee was next spotted, it was at the Little League field in the park. A Little League game had just ended. The Red Sox had won, but the big story was John McNab, who struck out sixteen batters to set a new Two Mills L.L. record.

McNab was a giant. He stood five feet eight and was said to weigh over a hundred and seventy pounds. He had to bring his birth certificate in to the League director to prove he was only twelve. And still most people didn't believe it.

The point is, the rest of the league was no match for McNab. It wouldn't have been so bad if he'd been a right-fielder, but he was a pitcher. And there was only one pitch he ever threw: a fastball.

Most of the batters never saw it; they just heard it whizzing past their noses. You could see their knees shaking from the stands. One poor kid stood there long enough to hear strike one go past, then threw up all over home plate.

It was still pretty light out, because when there are a lot of strikeouts, a game goes fast. And McNab was still on the mound, even though the official game was over. He figured he'd made baseball history, and he wanted to stretch it out as long as he could.

There were still about ten players around, Red Soxers and Green Soxers, and McNab was making them march up to the plate and take their swings. There was no catcher. The ball just zoomed to the backstop. When a kid struck out, he went back to the end of the line.

McNab was loving it. After each whiff, he laughed and bellowed the strikeout total. "Twenty-*six!* . . . Twenty-*seven!* . . . Twenty-*eight!* . . ." He was like a shark. He had the blood lust. The victims were hunched and trembling, walking the gangplank. "Thirty-*four!* . . . Thirty-*five!* . . ."

And then somebody new stepped up to the plate. Just a punky, runty little kid, no Red Sox or Green Sox uniform. Kind of scraggly. With a book, which he laid down on home plate. He scratched out a footing in the batter's box, cocked the bat on his shoulder, and stared at McNab.

McNab croaked from the mound, "Get outta there, runt. This is a Little League record. You ain't in Little League."

The kid walked away. Was he chickening out? No. He was lifting a red cap from the next batter in line. He put it on. He was back in the box.

McNab almost fell off the mound, he was laughing so hard. "Okay, runt. Number thirty-six coming up."

McNab fired. The kid swung. The batters in line automatically turned their eyes to the backstop, where the ball should be — but it wasn't there. It was in the air, riding on a beeline right out to McNab's head, the same line it came in on, only faster. McNab froze, then flinched, just in time. The ball missed his head but nipped the bill of his cap and sent it spinning like a flying saucer out to shortstop. The ball landed in the second-base dust and rolled all the way to the fence in center field.

Dead silence. Nobody moved.

McNab was gaping at the kid, who was still standing there all calm and cool, waiting for the next pitch. Finally a sort of grin slithered across McNab's lips. He roared: "Get my hat! Get the ball!"

Ten kids scrambled onto the field, bringing him the hat and ball. McNab had it figured now. He was so busy laughing at the runt, he lobbed him a lollipop and the runt got lucky and poled it.

This time McNab wasn't laughing. He fingered the ball, tips digging into the red stitching. He wound, he fired, he thought: *Man! That sucker's goin' so fast even I can hardly see it!* And then he was looking up, turning, following the flight of the ball, which finally came down to earth in deep left center field and bounced once to the fence.

More silence, except from someone who yelped "Yip —" then caught himself.

"Ball!" bellowed McNab.

He was handed the ball. He slammed his hat to the ground. His nostrils flared, he was breathing like a picadored bull. He windmilled, reared, lunged, fired . . .

This time the ball cleared the fence on the fly.

No more holding back. The other kids cheered. Somebody ran for the ball. They were anxious now for more.

Three more pitches. Three more home runs.

Pandemonium on the sidelines. It was raining red and green hats.

McNab couldn't stand it. The next time he threw, it was right at the kid's head. The kid ducked. McNab called, "Strike one!"

Next pitch headed for the kid's belt. The kid bent his stomach around the ball. "Steee-rike *two!*"

Strike three took dead aim at the kid's knees, and here was the kid, swooping back and at the same time swatting at the ball like a golfer teeing off. It was the craziest baseball swing you ever saw, but there was the ball smoking out to center field.

"Hold it, runt," snarled McNab. "I can't pitch right when I gotta wizz."

The kids on the sidelines made way as McNab stomped off the field, past the dugout and into the woods between the field and the creek. They waited a pretty long time, but they figured, well, McNab's wizz probably would last longer than a regular kid's. Might even make the creek rise.

At last McNab was back on the mound, fingering the ball in his glove, a demon's gleam in his eye. He wound up, fired, the ball headed for the plate, and — what's this? — a legball? — it's got legs — long legs pinwheeling toward the plate. It wasn't a ball at all, it was a frog, and McNab was on the mound cackling away, and the kid at the plate was bug-eyed. He'd never — *nobody'd* ever — tried to hit a fast*frog* before.

So what did the kid do? He *bunted* it. He bunted the frog, laid down a perfect bunt in front of the plate, third-base side, and he took off for first. He was half-way to second before McNab jolted himself into action. The kid was trying for an inside-the-park home-run bunt — the rarest feat in baseball, something that had hardly ever been done with a ball, and never with a frog — and to be the pitcher who let such a thing happen — well, McNab could already feel his strikeout record fading to a mere grain in the sandlot of history.

So he lumbered off the mound after the frog, which was now hopping down the third-base line. As a matter of fact, it was so close to the line that McNab had a brilliant idea — just herd the frog across the line and it would be a foul ball (or frog). Which is what he tried to do with his foot. But the frog, instead of taking a left turn at the shoe, jumped over it and hopped on toward third base. He was heading for the green fields of left, and the runt kid, sounding like two runners with his flap-soles slapping the bottoms of his feet, was chucking dust for third.

Only one hope now — McNab had to grab the frog and tag the runner out. But now the frog shot through his legs, over to the mound, and now toward shortstop and now toward second, and McNab was lurching and lunging, throwing his hat at the frog, throwing his glove, and everybody was screaming, and the kid was rounding third and digging for home, and — unbefroggable! — the "ball" was heading back home too! The ball, the batter, the pitcher all racing for home plate, and it was the batter, the new kid out of nowhere, who crossed the plate first, at the same time scooping up his book, twirling his borrowed red cap back to the cheering others, and jogging on past the empty stands and up the hill to the boulevard; McNab gasping, croaking after him: "Don't stop till yer outta town, runt! Don't let me ever catch ya!"

And that's how Jeffrey Magee knocked the world's first frogball for a four-bagger.

8

*A*nd how he came to be called Maniac.

The town was buzzing. The schools were buzzing. Hallways. Lunchrooms. Streets. Playgrounds. West End. East End.

Buzzing about the new kid in town. The stranger kid. Scraggly. Carrying a book. Flap-soled sneakers.

The kid who intercepted Brian Denehy's pass to Hands Down and punted it back longer than Denehy himself ever threw it.

The kid who rescued Arnold Jones from Finsterwald's backyard.

The kid who tattooed Giant John McNab's fastball for half a dozen home runs, then circled the sacks on a bunted frog.

Nobody knows who said it first, but somebody must have: "Kid's gotta be a maniac."

And somebody else must have said: "Yeah, reg'lar maniac."

And somebody else: "Yeah."

And that was it. Nobody (except Amanda Beale) had any other name for him, so pretty soon, when they wanted to talk about the new kid, that's what they called him: Maniac.

The legend had a name.

But not an address. At least, not an official one, with numbers.

What he did have was the deer shed at the Elmwood Park Zoo, which is where he slept his first few nights in town. What the deer ate, especially the carrots, apples, and day-old hamburger buns, he ate.

He started reading Amanda Beale's book his second day in town and finished it that afternoon. Ordinarily, he would have returned it immediately, but he was so fascinated by the story of the Children's Crusade that he kept it and read it the next day. And the next.

When he wasn't reading, he was wandering. When most people wander, they walk. Maniac Magee ran. Around town, around the nearby townships, always carrying the book, keeping it in perfect condition.

This is what he was doing when his life, as it often seemed to do, took an unexpected turn.

9

*J*ohn McNab had never in his life met a kid he couldn't strike out. Until the runt. Now, as he thought about it, he came to two conclusions:

1. He couldn't stand having this blemish on his record.

2. If you beat a kid up, it's the same as striking him out.

So McNab and his pals went looking for the kid. They called themselves the Cobras. Nobody messed with them. At least, nobody in the West End.

The Cobras had heard that the kid hung around the park and the tracks, and that's where they spotted him one Saturday afternoon, on the tracks by the path that ran from the Oriole Street dead end to the park. He was down by Red Hill and heading away from them, book in hand, as usual.

But the Cobras just stood there, stunned.

"I don't believe it," one Cobra said.

"Must be a trick," said another.

"I heard about it," said another, "but I didn't believe it."

It wasn't a trick. It was true. The kid was *running* on the rail.

McNab scooped up a handful of track stones. He launched one. He snarled, "He's dead. Let's get 'im!"

By the time Maniac looked back, they were almost on him. He wobbled once, leaped from the rail to the ground, and took off. He was at the Oriole Street dead end, but his instincts said no, not the street, too much open space. He stuck with the tracks. Coming into view above him was the house on Rako Hill, where he had eaten spaghetti. He could go there, to the whistling mother, the other kids, be safe. They wouldn't follow him in there. Would they?

Stones clanked off the steel rails. He darted left, skirted the dump, wove through the miniature mountain range of stone piles and into the trees . . . skiing on his heels down the steep bank and into the creek, frogs plopping, no time to look for stepping rocks . . . yells behind him now, war whoops, stones pelting the water, stinging his back . . . ah, the other side, through the trees and picker bushes, past the armory jeeps and out to the park boulevard, past the Italian restaurant on the corner, the bakery, screeching tires, row houses, streets, alleys, cars, porches, windows, faces staring, faces, faces . . . the town whizzing past Maniac, a blur of faces, each face staring from its own window, each face in its own personal frame, its own house, its own address, someplace to be when there was no other place to be, how lucky to be a face staring out from a window . . .

And then — could it be? — the voices behind him were growing faint. He slowed, turned, stopped. They were lined up at a street a block back. They were still yelling and shaking their fists, but they weren't moving off the curb. And now they were laughing. Why were they laughing?

The Cobras were standing at Hector Street. Hector Street was the boundary between the East and West Ends. Or, to put it another way, between the blacks and whites. Not that you never saw a white in the East End or a black in the West End. People did cross the line now and then, especially if they were adults, and it was daylight.

But nighttime, forget it. And if you were a kid, day *or* night, forget it. Unless you had business on the other side, such as a sports team or school. But don't be just *strolling* along, as if you *belonged* there, as if you weren't *afraid,* as if you didn't even *notice* you were a different color from everybody around you.

The Cobras were laughing because they figured the dumb, scraggly runt would get out of the East End in about as good shape as a bare big toe in a convention of snapping turtles.

10

Of course, Maniac didn't know any of that. He was simply glad the chase was over. He turned and started walking, catching his breath.

East Chestnut. East Marshall. Green Street. Arch Street. He had been around here before. That first day with the girl named Amanda, other days jogging through. But this was Saturday, not a school day, and there was something different about the streets — kids. All over.

One of them jumped down from a front step and planted himself right in front of Maniac. Maniac had to jerk to a stop to keep from plowing into the kid. Even so, their noses were practically touching.

Maniac blinked and stepped back. The kid stepped forward. Each time Maniac stepped back, the kid stepped forward. They traveled practically half a block that way. Finally Maniac turned and started walking. The kid jumped around and plunked himself in front again. He bit off a chunk of the candy bar he was holding. "Where *you* goin'?" he said. Candy bar flakes flew from his mouth.

"I'm looking for Sycamore Street," said Maniac. "Do you know where it is?"

"Yeah, I know where it is."

Maniac waited, but the kid said nothing more. "Well, uh, do you think you could tell me where it is?"

Stone was softer than the kid's glare. "No."

Maniac looked around. Other kids had stopped playing, were staring.

Someone called: "Do 'im, Mars!"

Someone else: "Waste 'im!"

The kid, as you probably guessed by now, was none other than Mars Bar Thompson. Mars Bar heard the calls, and the stone got harder. Then suddenly he stopped glaring, suddenly he was smiling. He held up the candy bar, an inch from Maniac's lips. "Wanna bite?"

Maniac couldn't figure. "You sure?"

"Yeah, go ahead. Take a bite."

Maniac shrugged, took the Mars Bar, bit off a chunk, and handed it back. "Thanks."

Dead silence along the street. The kid had done the unthinkable, he had chomped on one of Mars's own bars. Not only that, but white kids just didn't put their mouths where black kids had had theirs, be it soda bottles, spoons, or candy bars. And the kid hadn't even gone for the unused end; he had chomped right over Mars Bar's own bite marks.

Mars Bar was confused. Who *was* this kid? *What* was this kid?

As usual, when Mars Bar got confused, he got mad. He thumped Maniac in the chest. "You think you bad or somethin'?"

Maniac, who was now twice as confused as Mars Bar, blinked. "Huh?"

"You think you come down here and be bad? That what you think?" Mars Bar was practically shouting now.

"No," said Maniac, "I don't think I'm bad. I'm not saying I'm an angel, either. Not even real good. Somewhere in between, I guess."

Mars Bar jammed his arms downward, stuck out his chin, sneered. "Am I bad?"

Maniac was befuddled. "*I* don't know. One minute you're yelling at me, the next minute you're giving me a bite of your candy bar."

The chin jutted out more. "Tell me I'm bad."

Maniac didn't answer. Flies stopped buzzing.

"I said, tell me I'm bad."

Maniac blinked, shrugged, sighed. "It's none of my business. If you're bad, let your mother or father tell you."

Now it was Mars Bar doing the blinking, stepping back, trying to sort things out. After a while he looked down. "What's that?"

Before Maniac answered, "A book," Mars Bar had snatched it from his hand. "This ain't yours," he said. He flipped through some pages. "Looks like mine."

"It's somebody else's."

"It's mine. I'm keepin' it."

With rattlesnake speed, Maniac snatched the book back — except for one page, which stayed, ripped, in Mars Bar's hand.

"Give me the page," said Maniac.

Mars Bar grinned. "Take it, fishbelly."

Silence. Eyes. The flies were waiting. East End vultures.

Suddenly neither kid could see the other, because a broom came down like a straw curtain between their faces, and a voice said, "*I'll* take it."

It was the lady from the nearest house, out to sweep her steps. She lowered the broom but kept it between them. "Better yet," she said to Mars Bar, "just give it back to him."

Mars Bar glared up at her. There wasn't an eleven-year-old in the East End who could stand up to Mars Bar's glare. In the West End, even high-schoolers were known to crumble under the glare. To old ladies on both sides of Hector Street, it was all but fatal. And when Mars Bar stepped off a curb and combined the glare with his super-slow dip-stride slumpshuffle, well, it was said he could back up traffic all the way to Bridgeport while he took ten minutes to cross the street.

But not this time. This time Mars Bar was up against an East End lady in her prime, and she was matching him eyeball for eyeball. And when it was over, only one glare was left standing, and it wasn't Mars Bar's.

Mars Bar handed back the torn page, but not before he crumpled it into a ball. The broom pushed him away, turned him around, and swept him up the street.

The lady looked down at Maniac. A little of the glare lingered in her eyes. "You better get on, boy, where you belong. I can't be following you around. I got things to do."

Maniac just stood there a minute. There was something he felt like doing, and maybe he would have, but the lady turned and went back inside her house and shut the door. So he walked away.

11

*N*ow what?

Maniac uncrumpled the page, flattened it out as best he could. How could he return the book to Amanda in this condition? He couldn't. But he had to. It was hers. Judging from that morning, she was pretty finicky about her books. What would make her madder — to not get the book back at all, or to get it back with a page ripped out? Maniac cringed at both prospects.

He wandered around the East End, jogging slowly, in no hurry now to find 728 Sycamore Street. He was passing a vacant lot when he heard an all-too-familiar voice: "Hey, fishbelly!" He stopped, turned. This time Mars Bar wasn't alone. A handful of other kids trailed him down the sidewalk.

Maniac waited.

Coming up to him, Mars Bar said, "Where you runnin', boy?"

"Nowhere."

"You runnin' from us. You afraid."

"No, I just like to run."

"You wanna run?" Mars Bar grinned. "Go ahead. We'll give you a head start."

Maniac grinned back. "No thanks."

Mars Bar held out his hand. "Gimme my book."

Maniac shook his head.

Mars Bar glared. "Gimme it."

Maniac shook his head.

Mars Bar reached for it. Maniac pulled it away.

They moved in on him now. They backed him up. Some high-schoolers were playing basketball up the street, but they weren't noticing. And there wasn't a broom-swinging lady in sight. Maniac felt a hard flatness against his back. Suddenly his world was very small and very simple: a brick wall behind him, a row of scowling faces in front of him. He clutched the book with both hands. The faces were closing in. A voice called: "That you, Jeffrey?"

The faces parted. At the curb was a girl on a bike — Amanda! She hoisted the bike to the sidewalk and walked it over. She looked at the book, at the torn page. "Who ripped my book?"

Mars Bar pointed at Maniac. "He did."

Amanda knew better. "*You* ripped my book."

Mars Bar's eyes went big as headlights. "I did *not!*"

"You *did.* You lie."

"I *didn't!*"

"You *did!*" She let the bike fall to Maniac. She grabbed the book and started kicking Mars Bar in his beloved sneakers. "I got a little brother and a little sister that crayon all over my books, and I got a dog that eats them and poops on them and that's just inside my own family, and I'm *not* — gonna have *nobody* — else *messin'* — with my *books!* You under-*stand?*"

By then Mars Bar was hauling on up the street past the basketball players, who were rolling on the asphalt with laughter.

Amanda took the torn page from Maniac. To her, it was the broken wing of a bird, a pet out in the rain. She turned misty eyes to Maniac. "It's one of my favorite pages."

Maniac smiled. "We can fix it."

The way he said it, she believed. "Want to come to my house?" she said.

"Sure," he said.

12

*W*hen they walked in, Amanda's mother was busy with her usual tools: a yellow plastic bucket and a sponge. She was scrubbing purple crayon off the TV screen.

"Mom," said Amanda, "this is Jeffrey —" She whispered, "What's your last name?"

He whispered, "Magee."

She said, "Magee."

Mrs. Beale held up a hand, said, "Hold it," and went on scrubbing. When she finally finished, she straightened up, turned, and said, "Now, what?"

"Mom, this is Jeffrey Magee. You know."

Amanda was hardly finished when Maniac zipped across the room and stuck out his hand. "Nice to meet you, Mrs. . . . Mrs. . . . ."

"Beale."

"Mrs. Beale."

They shook hands. Mrs. Beale smiled. "So you're the book boy." She started nodding. "Manda came home one day — 'Mom, there's a boy I loaned one of my books out to!' 'Loaned a *book? You?*' 'Mom, he practically *made* me. He really likes books. I met him on —' "

"Mo-om!" Amanda screeched. "I never said all *that!*"

Mrs. Beale nodded solemnly — "No, of course you didn't" — and gave Maniac a huge wink, which made Amanda screech louder, until something crashed in the kitchen. Mrs. Beale ran. Amanda and Maniac ran.

The scene in the kitchen stopped them cold: one little girl, eyes wide, standing on a countertop; one little boy, eyes wide, standing just below her on a chair; one shattered glass jar and some stringy pale-colored glop on the floor; one growing cloud of sauerkraut fumes.

The girl was Hester, age four; the boy was Lester, age three. In less than five minutes, while Mrs. Beale and Amanda cleaned up the floor, Hester and Lester and their dog Bow Wow were in the backyard wrestling and tickling and jumping and just generally going wild with their new buddy — and victim — Maniac Magee.

Maniac was still there when Mr. Beale came home from his Saturday shift at the tire factory.

He was there for dinner, when Hester and Lester pushed their chairs alongside his.

He was there to help Amanda mend her torn book.

He was there watching TV afterward, with Hester riding one knee, Lester the other.

He was there when Hester and Lester came screaming down the stairs with a book, Amanda screaming even louder after them, the kids shoving the book and themselves onto Maniac's lap, Amanda finally calming down because they didn't want to crayon the book, they only wanted Maniac to read. And so he read *Lyle, Lyle, Crocodile* to Hester and Lester and, even though they pretended not to listen, to Amanda and Mr. and Mrs. Beale.

And he was there when Hester and Lester were herded upstairs to bed, and Mrs. Beale said, "Don't you think it's about time you're heading home, Jeffrey? Your parents'll be wondering."

So Maniac, wanting to say something but not knowing how, got into the car for Mr. Beale to drive him home. And then he made his mistake. He waited for only two or three blocks to go by before saying to Mr. Beale, "This is it."

Mr. Beale stopped, but he didn't let Maniac out of the car. He looked at him funny. Mr. Beale knew what his passenger apparently didn't: East End was East End and West End was West End, and the house this white lad was pointing to was filled with black people, just like every other house on up to Hector Street.

Mr. Beale pointed this out to Maniac. Maniac's lip started to quiver, and right there, with the car idling in the middle of the street, Maniac told him that he didn't really have a home, unless you counted the deer shed at the zoo.

Mr. Beale made a U-turn right there and headed back. Only Mrs. Beale was still downstairs when they walked into the house. She listened to no more than ten seconds' worth of Mr. Beale's explanation before saying to Maniac, "You're staying here."

Not long after, Maniac was lying in Amanda's bed, Amanda having been carried over to Hester and Lester's room, where she often slept anyway.

Before Maniac could go to sleep, however, there was something he had to do. He flipped off the covers and went downstairs. Before the puzzled faces of Mr. and Mrs. Beale, he opened the front door and looked at the three cast-iron digits nailed to the door frame: seven two eight. He kept staring at them, smiling. Then he closed the door, said a cheerful "Goodnight," and went back to bed.

Maniac Magee finally had an address.

13

Amanda was happy to give up her room to Maniac. It gave her an excuse to sleep with Hester and Lester every night. Most of the time during the day the little ones drove her crazy; she couldn't stand to be in the same hemisphere with them. But at night, the best thing was to have them snuggled up on both sides of her. It made no sense, but that's how it was.

Mr. Beale divided the little ones' room into two sections with a panel of plywood, and Amanda moved her stuff into the back part. Except for her suitcase of books — that stayed in her old room, with Maniac.

The way Maniac fit in, you would have thought he was born there.

He played with the little ones and read them stories and taught them things. He took Bow Wow out for runs and he did the dishes without anybody asking. (Which made Amanda feel guilty, so she started to dry.)

He carried out the trash, mowed the grass, cleaned

up his own spills, turned out lights, put the cap back on the toothpaste tube, flushed the toilet, and — Mrs. Beale called it "the miracle on Sycamore Street" — he kept his room neat.

Every morning Mrs. Beale looked into it. No socks on the floor, no drawers open, no messed-up bed. That was the most amazing thing, the bed. It looked as if it hadn't even been slept in. Which, she soon found out, was the case.

Late one night she opened the door and found Maniac sleeping on the floor. She lugged him onto the bed, but by the next night he was back on the floor. Maniac just couldn't stand being too comfortable. Lying on a mattress gave him a weird feeling of slowly rising on a scoop of mashed potatoes.

He was that way with chairs too. If he had a choice, he usually sat on the floor.

Other strange things happened in the house.

Such as: the yellow bucket and sponge spent more time gathering dust in the cellar and less time in Mrs. Beale's hands. Because, with Maniac around, Hester and Lester lost their interest in crayoning everything in sight. And therefore, sometimes for fifteen minutes in a row, Mrs. Beale was seen doing something she hadn't done since the little ones were born: nothing.

Such as: Amanda started leaving her suitcase of books home.

Such as: everybody's fingertips started to heal. Because Maniac took over the endless, thankless job of untying Hester and Lester's sneaker knots.

Such as: Hester and Lester started to enjoy taking

a bath. Which was the solution to a very huge problem in the Beale household.

Once upon a time, Hester and Lester loved to get a bath — as long as Amanda got one with them. It was a little crowded, especially when the little ones added their boats and floating dinosaurs, but it was fun and warm and yelpy and soapy.

Then came the day when Amanda entered fourth grade, and she decided she was getting too old to tub it with her little brother and sister. They begged her and begged her, but she wouldn't get in. They tried to storm the bathroom when she was in there, but she locked the door on them.

And so the little ones went on strike. They placed their hands on *Lyle, Lyle, Crocodile* and swore they would never take another bath until Amanda joined them.

And even though they couldn't stop their much larger mother from lifting them up and plunking them into the water, they *could* refuse to touch the soap or washcloth. They could make her do it. And they could sit there all stiff with their chins down in their chests and their arms folded tightly and their legs clamped together. And if their mother wanted to wash their armpits, she would have to get a crowbar and pry their arms up, because they sure as heck were not going to move.

That's the way it was for a long time, until Maniac arrived.

On that first Sunday, as soon as the little ones found out that their new pal had slept over, they mobbed him: "Jeffrey! Jeffrey! Get a bath with us! Will ya?"

Maniac replied, "Sure, okay," not thinking much about it. After all, it was still before breakfast.

But the little ones never let up, and at exactly 9:15 A.M., the three of them got into the tub. By the time they got out, it was too late to go to church and almost lunchtime.

From then on, the baths usually took place at night. Sometimes Mrs. Beale would poke her head in and stare: one little black girl, one little black boy, one medium white boy. And she would smile and wag her head and sigh: "Never saw such a tub."

The time she heard Hester and Lester yelling for help, though, she was downstairs. She came running. "What's the matter?"

The little ones pointed. "Look!"

She looked. Maniac was covered with blotches — round, red blotches, all shiny from the bath water. They looked something like little pepperonis.

They took him to the doctor. The doctor took a look and said it wasn't chicken pox and it wasn't measles. He said it might be an allergy. He asked what the boy had had for dinner.

Mrs. Beale answered. "Pizza."

"Well!" The doctor chuckled. "Can't be that. Can you imagine a youngster getting sick on pizza?"

Everybody laughed.

"Besides," said the doctor, "this would have shown up on him since he was little, most likely, every time he came near a pizza." He turned to Maniac, still chuckling. "You *have* eaten pizza before, haven't you?"

Maniac got a funny expression on his face. He looked around. Everybody was staring at him. The silence grew longer, eyes grew wider . . .

And that's how they found out that Maniac Magee was allergic to pizza.

14

*M*aniac loved his new life.

He loved his new sneakers, the ones Mrs. Beale bought for him.

He loved the new quietness of his footsteps as he trotted Bow Wow through the early morning streets.

He loved the early morning. The "before-the-workingpeople time," he called it. When even those who went to work the earliest were still sleeping behind their second-story shades. When it seemed as if the whole world had been created just before he woke up on his bedroom floor — the red brick rows of houses, even the windows resting from faces, the cool, silent sidewalks and streets. So quiet you could hear the water running far below the sewer grates while the sun shinnied up the rainspouts.

He loved the silence and solitude.

But he also loved the noise, which came later in the day.

He loved the sound of pancake batter hissing on the griddle.

He loved the noise of the church they went to on Sunday mornings, a church called Bethany — when the minister would thump on the pulpit and the people would call out "Amen" and the choir would swing this way and swing that way and would sing "Hallelujah!" to the people and the people would sing "Hallelujah!" right back to the choir, and everyone just got happier and happier, and it all made him want to do more than run. So one day he just jumped himself up onto the pew bench and threw his arms to the sky and shouted at the top of his lungs: "Hallelujah! Amen!" And this time nobody looked funny at the crazy kid yelling by himself. Then two members of his own family, Hester and Lester, jumped onto the bench with him and shouted away: "Hallelujah! A-*men*!" And everybody laughed and clapped and sang.

He loved the Fourth of July block party, when the whole East End converged for a day and night of games and music and grilled chicken and ribs and sweet-potato pie and dancing until the last firecracker, and then some.

Maniac loved the colors of the East End, the people colors.

For the life of him, he couldn't figure why these East Enders called themselves black. He kept looking and looking, and the colors he found were gingersnap and light fudge and dark fudge and acorn and butter rum and cinnamon and burnt orange. But never licorice, which, to him, was real black.

He especially loved the warm brown of Mrs. Beale's thumb, as it appeared from under the creamy white icing that she allowed him to lick away when she was frosting his favorite cake.

He loved joining all the colors at the vacant lot and playing the summer days away. Stickball, basketball, football. Half the time he forgot to go home for lunch.

One day a new kid, tall and lean, came to the vacant lot, spinning a football. He spotted Maniac and stopped cold. He came closer, bent over, stared. Then he broke open a billboard grin and called out, "Hey, everybody! 'Member I said 'bout the little white dude snatched the pass off me in gym class? Here he is. This is the dude!"

And this, of course, was Hands Down.

The first thing Hands did, when they chose up sides, was to pick Maniac for his team.

"You crazy, Hands," a high-schooler laughed. "He's just a runt. His peach fuzz ain't even come in yet."

Everybody laughed.

But Hands took him anyway and played quarter-back and threw passes to Maniac all day long. They huddled and scratched their plays in the dirt. Down to the tin can and break for the goal. Stop and go at the rock. Curl around the junked tire.

If Hands's pass was anywhere near Maniac, if Maniac could get at least two fingertips on it, the ball was good as caught. The high-schoolers and junior-highers went crazy trying to stop him. Nobody kept official records that day, but legend has it that by the time Amanda Beale showed up and called, "Jeffrey — dinner!" Maniac had scored forty-nine TDs.

And when they played stickball, and they saw him

poling the ball out to the street and into backyards, they started putting two and two together, and somebody came up to him and squinted in his face and said, "You that Maniac kid?"

And somebody else said, "You that Maniac?"

And pretty soon everybody was saying it, including Hester and Lester; and, finally, in the kitchen one day, as he licked white icing from her thumb, Mrs. Beale said it: "You that Maniac?"

He told her what he told everyone. "I'm Jeffrey. You know me." Because he was afraid of losing his name, and with it the only thing he had left from his mother and father.

Mrs. Beale smiled. "Yeah, I know you all right. You'll be nothing but Jeffrey in here. But —" she nodded to the door — "out there, I don't know."

She was right, of course. Inside his house, a kid gets one name, but on the other side of the door, it's whatever the rest of the world wants to call him.

15

*M*aniac's fame spread all over the East End. The new white kid.

Who lived with the Beales at 728 Sycamore.

Who ran the streets before the fathers went out.

Who could poleax a stickball like a twelfth-grader and catch a football like Hands Down.

Who was allergic to pizza.

Who jumped up in Bethany Church and shouted, "Hallelujah! A-*men!*"

Little kids, especially preschoolers, came from all over, bringing him their knots. They had heard about him from Hester and Lester. They had heard he could untie a sneaker knot quicker than a kid could spend a quarter.

The bigger kids came around too, for other reasons. From Moore Street and Arch Street and Chestnut and Green. Heading for the vacant lot to check out the new kid. To test him. To see if everything they'd heard was true. To see how good he really was. And how bad.

They found out he could do more with a football than just catch it. He could run like a squirrel. He juked and jived and spun and danced and darted, and he left them squeezing handfuls of air. Pretty soon the vacant lot was littered with blown sneakers and broken hearts.

He didn't do much talking, but he didn't have to. Hands Down did it for him.

Every time he scored a TD or cracked a home run, Hands was bent over in his face, talking trash. "Do it, man! Smoke them suckas! Poke 'em! Joke 'em! You bad-dudin' it! You the baddest! Five me, jude!"

And they high-fived and low-fived and back-fived, and Hands Down would laugh and laugh.

Maniac loved trash talk. The words were different, but in some strange way they reminded him of church. It had spirit, it had what they called soul. Pretty soon he was talking trash with the rest of them.

And pretty soon he brought it home.

Mrs. Beale was pressing her famous meatloaf into a baking pan one day, when Maniac started talking his trash to her. Her eyes shot open. She straightened up. "Wha'd you say?"

He said some more.

At first she couldn't believe her ears. When she did believe them, she didn't like it. She didn't like this boy bringing the vacant lot into her kitchen, and she didn't like how it fit his mouth. So she put a stop to it right then and there and slapped that trash-talking mouth.

Her lip started to quiver before his, but before she could say "I'm sorry," he was hugging and squeezing her and burying his face in her chest and sobbing, "I love you . . . I love you . . ."

And he loved the quiet times after Hester and Lester went to bed. That's when he read Amanda's books. When he had gone through about half of them, he figured it was time to tackle the encyclopedia A.

Problem was, Amanda was always reading it. And she vowed she wasn't giving it up, not even to Maniac, till she read everything from Aardvark to Aztec. To make matters worse, the supermarket offer had expired, so there were no other volumes.

The more Amanda would not let go of the A, the more Maniac wanted it. It reached the point where she had to hide it whenever she wasn't reading it. Unbeknownst to her, Maniac always found it. He would get up even *earlier* in the morning, read it by flashlight for a while, sneak it back, and go trotting with Bow Wow.

And sometimes Maniac just sat at the front window, being on the inside.

Maniac loved almost everything about his new life.

But everything did not love him back.

16

*M*aniac Magee was blind. Sort of.

Oh, he could see objects, all right. He could see a flying football or a John McNab fastball better than anybody.

He could see Mars Bar's foot sticking out, trying to trip him up as he circled the bases for a home run.

He could see Mars Bar charging from behind to tackle him, even when he didn't have the football.

He could see Mars Bar's bike veering for a nearby puddle to splash water on him.

He could see these things, but he couldn't see what they meant. He couldn't see that Mars Bar disliked him, maybe even hated him.

When you think about it, it's amazing all the stuff he didn't see.

Such as, big kids don't like little kids showing them up.

And big kids like it even less if another big kid (such as Hands Down) is laughing at them while the little kid is faking them out of their Fruit of the Looms.

And some kids don't like a kid who is different.

Such as a kid who is allergic to pizza.

Or a kid who does dishes without being told.

Or a kid who never watches Saturday morning cartoons.

Or a kid who's another color.

Maniac kept trying, but he still couldn't see it, this color business. He didn't figure he was white any more than the East Enders were black. He looked himself over pretty hard and came up with at least seven different shades and colors right on his own skin, not one of them being what he would call white (except for his eyeballs, which weren't any whiter than the eyeballs of the kids in the East End).

Which was all a big relief to Maniac, finding out he wasn't really white, because the way he figured, white was about the most boring color of all.

But there it was, piling up around him: dislike. Not from everybody. But enough. And Maniac couldn't see it.

And then all of a sudden he could.

17

*I*t was a hot day in August.

It was so hot, if you stood still too long in the vacant lot, the sun bouncing off a chunk of broken glass or metal could fry a patch on your hide.

So hot, if you were packing candy, you had soup in your pocket by two o'clock.

So hot, the dogs were tripping on their own tongues.

And so hot, the fire hydrant at Green and Chestnut was gushing like Niagara Falls (courtesy of somebody wrenching off the cap).

By the time Maniac and the rest of the vacant lot regulars got there, Chestnut and Green was a cross between a block party and a swimming pool. Radios blaring. People blaring. Somebody selling lemonade. Somebody selling Kool-Aid ice cubes on toothpicks. Bodies. Skin. Colors. Water. Gleaming. Buttery. Warm. Cool. Wet. Screaming. Happy.

The younger you were, the fewer clothes you had

on. Grownups sat on the sidewalk and dangled their
bare feet in the running gutters. Teenagers stripped
down to bathing suits and cutoffs. Little kids, under-
wear. Littlest kids, nothing.

Maniac danced and pranced and screamed with the
rest. He learned how to jump in front of the gusher
and let it propel him halfway across the street. He
joined in a snake dance. He got goofy. He drenched
himself in all the wet and warm and happy.

When he first heard the voice, he didn't think much
of it. Just one voice, one voice in hundreds. But then
the other voices were falling away, in bunches, until
only this one was left. It was a strange voice, deep
and thick and sort of clotted, as though it had to fight
its way through a can of worms before coming out.
The voice was behind him, saying the same word over
and over . . . calling . . . a name . . . and even then
Maniac turned only because he was curious, wondering what everybody was staring at. But when he saw
the brown finger pointed at him (not a speck of icing
on it), and the brown arm that aimed it and the brown
face behind it, he knew the name coming out of the
can-of-worms mouth was his: "Whitey." And it surprised him that he knew.

He just stood there, blinking through the water-
drop sun blur, the hydrant gusher smacking his thin,
bare ankles. The radios, the people, were silent.

"You move on now, Whitey," the man said. "You
pick up your gear and move on out. Time to go home
now."

The man was close enough to be catching some

water around his shoes, which, Maniac noticed, were actually slippers. His pants were baggy, and his shirt wasn't really a shirt but a pajama top covered with high-tailed roosters. White hair curled around his ears.

Maniac gave his answer: "I *am* home."

The man took a step closer, dropped his arm. "You go on home now, son. Back to your own kind. I seen ya at the block party. Now you get goin'."

Maniac stepped out of the gusher, the water roared on to the opposite curb. "This *is* where I live. I live right down there." He pointed toward Sycamore.

The man didn't seem to notice. "Never enough, is it, Whitey? Just want more and more. Won't even leave us our little water in the street. Come on down to see Bojangles. Come on to the zoo. The monkey house."

He must be hard of hearing, Maniac thought. So he called it out really loud and slow and pointed again. "I — live — at — seven — twenty — eight — Sy — ca — more. I — do."

The old man stepped closer. "You got your own kind. It's how you wanted it. Let's keep it that way. NOW MOVE ON. Your kind's waitin' " — he flung his finger westward — "up there."

Suddenly Hester and Lester were by Maniac's side, barking at the man. "You leave him alone, Old Ragpicker! You shut up!"

And the man was croaking, ranting, not to Maniac now but to the people. "What happens when *we* go over *there?* Black is black! White is white! The sheep lie not with the lion! The sheep knows his own! His own kind!" A woman was rushing in then, pulling him away, up the street. "Our own kind! . . . our own kind! . . ."

The water thundered across the silent street.

Maniac, who was one of the world's great sleepers, didn't sleep well that night. Or the next.

He started getting up earlier than usual, not to sneak some time with the A book — just to run. Bow Wow wasn't even ready for his morning pee yet, but he went along.

Usually Maniac just jogged around the East End; now he did the whole town, plus over the river to Bridgeport. By the third day, Bow Wow refused to go along.

One morning, as Maniac was heading home, Hester and Lester came running up Sycamore. "Maniac! C'mon! *We're* gonna run too! Let's go *that* way!"

They tried to turn him around, but he told them to just hold on a minute; he wanted to stop home for a quick drink, then he'd go running with them. They kept yelling and tugging and pushing and grabbing his legs. And then Amanda was pedaling frantically up to him, slapping on a quick smile and gasping, "Hey, I'm going to the store. Wanna come along?"

Maniac checked the sun. It was hardly up to the second stories. "Stores aren't open yet," he said.

Amanda just gawked. She was a rotten liar, Maniac knew. He shook loose from the little ones and trotted on. He didn't know what, but something was wrong.

The little ones jabbered and screeched and grabbed. He ran faster, faster . . .

Mrs. Beale was out front with the yellow bucket, soapsuds spilling over the brim, a stiff bristle brush in her hand. She was scrubbing the house, the brick wall, scrubbing furiously at the chalk, grunting with the effort, her cheeks wet. He had been way too early, way too fast. Only the *F* had been scrubbed away. The rest was quite easy to read, the tall yellow letters the same color as the scrub bucket:

ISHBELLY GO HOME

18

Amanda tried to reason with him. "You can't listen to that old coot. He's goofy. He's always saying stuff like that. You can't go because of something one nutty old coot says."

Maniac pointed out that it wasn't the nutty old coot who chalked up the front of the house.

Amanda laughed. "*That?* That's no big deal. It wasn't even paint. If they really meant it, they would've done it in paint. And anyway, don't you know they did my mother a favor? It gave her a chance to get out the old bucket and do some serious scrubbing. Ever since the kids stopped crayoning the house, she hasn't known what to do with herself. Now she's happy again."

Maniac didn't answer. Amanda didn't understand that most of the hurt he felt was not for himself but for her and the rest of the family. She stomped her foot. "You *gotta* stay!"

"I don't *gotta* do anything."

"You go, you'll starve."

"Was I starving before I came here?"

"You'll freeze to death in the winter. Your fingers'll get so stiff they'll break off like icicles."

"I'll go somewhere."

"*Some*where? Like the deer pen?"

"I'll be okay."

"Or maybe Prairie Dog Town, huh? How about that?" She jabbed him. "You could live in a gopher hole. You'd be starving, so that would be perfect, because then you'd be so skinny you could fit right down there all snuggly in their little tunnels."

He shrugged. "Sounds cozy."

This was driving Amanda bonkers. He was acting so different, all glum, and wiseacre answers. As if he didn't care, not about anything.

"Yeah?" she sniffed. "Well, what're you gonna do for a pillow, huh? I *know* you put *my* pillow on the floor."

"I'll use a hibernating gopher."

"Fuh-nee. And bathroom, huh? Where will you go to the bathroom?"

"The bushes. McDonald's. Lots of places."

She hated it. An answer for everything. And the scariest part was, he was probably right. If anybody could survive on the loose, it would be this kid who showed up from Hollidaysburg. Who slept on floors. Who outran dogs.

He was making her so *mad!*

She pointed at him, she sneered, "Well, I'll tell you one thing, buddy boy. You better shut the door on your way out and lock it, because if I get my room back, I'm not giving it up again. So don'r crawling back around here." She kicked him in the sneaker. "You *hear?*"

"Don't worry," he said flatly.

"And don't think you're taking any of my *books* with you this time, either. And you can forget about — *ever* — getting a chance to open my encyclopedia A, which I was almost ready to let you do before you went and started *acting* all *poopy.*"

He said, "I'll join the library."

She jumped up. "Hah! You can't."

"No?"

"No. You need a library card."

"I'll get one."

"Hah-*hah!* You *can't* get a library card without an *address!*"

She regretted it as soon as she said it. His head swung, his eyes met hers. His eyes said, *Why did you say that?* Her eyes couldn't answer.

He got up and went out and trotted up the street.

Amanda cried. She tore a magazine in half. She punched the sofa. She kicked the easy chair. She kicked Bow Wow. Bow Wow went yelping into the kitchen. "See!" she yelled at the front door. "See what you made me do, Jeffrey Magee! Jeffrey Maniac Crazy Man Bozo Magee!"

He wasn't back by lunch.

He wasn't back by dinner.

"I'm going looking," Amanda told her worried parents. No one tried to stop her.

She rode her bike all over. East End. West End.

She even went over to Bridgeport, practically got herself killed on the bridge. She never pedaled so much in her life. She didn't come home till after dark.

When her parents headed upstairs to bed, she asked if she could stay up to watch TV. They looked at each other and said okay. She was nodding off in the middle of some late, late movie when the door opened and in he walked.

"What're you doing up so late?" he said.

"I'm incubating an egg," she snarled.

He shrugged and went upstairs. She closed her eyes and smiled.

Next morning a little kid from three blocks away came knocking at the front door. His yo-yo string had a knot fat as a mushroom.

As Amanda watched Maniac tackle the knot, an idea slithered into her brain. When the little kid left with his string good as new, she said, "Jeffrey, if I knew some way that would make it okay for you to stay, would you?"

"What do you mean 'okay'?" he said.

"I mean, that even if there's one or two people who aren't too wild about you now — and that's all there really are — that even *they* would like you. And everybody else who *already* likes you, they'll like you even *more*."

Purely out of curiosity, Maniac replied, "How's all that supposed to happen?"

Amanda told him about Cobble's Knot.

19

*I*f the Wonders of the World hadn't stopped at seven, Cobble's Knot would have been number eight.

Nobody knew how it got there. As the story goes, the original Mr. Cobble wasn't doing too well with the original Cobble's Corner Grocery at the corner of Hector and Birch. In his first two weeks, all he sold was some Quaker Oats and penny candy.

Then one morning, as he unlocked the front door for business, he saw the Knot. It was dangling from the flagpole that hung over the big picture window, the one that said FROSTED FOODS in icy blue-and-white letters. He got out a pair of scissors and was about to snip it off, when he noticed what an unusual and incredible knot it was.

And then he got an idea. He could offer a prize to anyone who untangled the Knot. Publicize it. Call the newspaper. Winner's picture on the front page, Cobble's Corner in the background. Business would boom.

Well, he went ahead and did it, and if business didn't exactly boom, it must have at least peeped a little, because eons later, when Maniac Magee came to town,

Cobble's Corner was still there. Only now it sold pizza instead of groceries. And the prize was different. It had started out being sixty seconds alone with the candy counter; now it was one large pizza per week for a whole year.

Which, in time, made the Knot practically priceless. Which is why, after leaving it outside for a year, Mr. Cobble took it down and kept it in a secret place inside the store and brought it out only to meet a challenger.

If you look at old pictures in the *Two Mills Times,* you see that the Knot was about the size and shape of a lopsided volleyball. It was made of string, but it had more contortions, ins and outs, twists and turns and dips and doodles than the brain of Albert Einstein himself. It had defeated all comers for years, including J.J. Thorndike, who grew up to be a magician, and Fingers Halloway, who grew up to be a pickpocket.

Hardly a week went by without somebody taking a shot at the Knot, and losing. And each loser added to the glory that awaited someone who could untie it.

"So you see," said Amanda, "if you go up there and untie Cobble's Knot — which I *know* you can — you'll get your picture in the paper and you'll be the biggest hero ever around here and *nooo*-body'll mess with you then."

Maniac listened and thought about it and finally gave a little grin. "Maybe you're just after the pizza, since you know I can't eat it."

Amanda screeched. "Jeff-*freee!* The pizza's not the point." She started to hit him. He laughed and grabbed her wrists. And he said okay, he'd give it a try.

20

*T*hey brought out the Knot and hung it from the flagpole. They brought out the official square wooden table for the challenger to stand on, and from the moment Maniac climbed up, you could tell the Knot was in big trouble.

To the ordinary person, Cobble's Knot was about as friendly as a nest of yellowjackets. Besides the tangle itself, there was the weathering of that first year, when the Knot hung outside and became hard as a rock. You could barely make out the individual strands. It was grimy, moldy, crusted over. Here and there a loop stuck out, maybe big enough to stick your pinky finger through, pitiful testimony to the challengers who had tried and failed.

And there stood Maniac, turning the Knot, checking it out. Some say there was a faint grin on his face, kind of playful, as though the Knot wasn't his enemy at all, but an old pal just playing a little trick on him. Others say his mouth was more grim than grin, that his eyes lit up like flashbulbs, because he knew he was finally facing a knot that would stand up and fight, a worthy opponent.

He lifted it in his hands to feel the weight of it. He touched it here and touched it there, gently, daintily. He scraped a patch of crust off with his fingernail. He laid his fingertips on it, as though feeling for a pulse.

Only a few people were watching at first, and half of them were Heck's Angels, a roving tricycle gang of four- and five-year-olds. Most of them had had sneaker-lace or yo-yo knots untied by Maniac, and they expected this would only take a couple of seconds longer. When the seconds became minutes, they started to get antsy, and before ten minutes had passed, they were zooming off in search of somebody to terrorize.

The rest of the spectators watched Maniac poke and tug and pick at the knot. Never a big pull or yank, just his fingertips touching and grazing and peck-pecking away, like some little bird.

"What's he doin'?" somebody said.

"What's taking so long?"

"He gonna do it or not?"

After an hour, except for a few more finger-size loops, all Maniac had to show for his trouble were the flakes of knot crust that covered the table.

"He ain't even found the end of the string yet," somebody grumbled, and almost everybody but Amanda took off.

Maniac never noticed. He just went on working.

By lunchtime they were all back, and more kept

coming. Not only kids, but grownups, too, black and white, because Cobble's Corner was on Hector, and word was racing through the neighborhoods on both the east and west sides of the street.

What people saw they didn't believe.

The knot had grown, swelled, exploded. It was a frizzy globe — the newspaper the next day described it as a "gigantic hairball." Now, except for a packed-in clump at the center, it was practically all loops. You could look through it and see Maniac calmly working on the other side.

"He found the end!" somebody gasped, and the corner burst into applause.

Meanwhile, inside, Cobble's was selling pizza left and right, not to mention zeps (a Two Mills type of hoagie), steak sandwiches, strombolis, and gallons of soda. Mr. Cobble himself came out to offer Maniac some pizza, which Maniac of course politely turned down. He did accept an orange soda, though, and then a little kid, whose sneaker laces Maniac had untied many a time, handed up to him a three-pack of Tastykake butterscotch Krimpets.

After polishing off the Krimpets, Maniac did the last thing anybody expected: he lay down and took a nap right there on the table, the knot hanging above him like a small hairy planet, the mob buzzing all around him. Maniac knew what the rest of them didn't: the hardest part was yet to come. He had to find the right routes to untangle the mess, or it would just close up again like a rock and probably stay that way forever. He would need the touch of a surgeon, the alertness of an owl, the cunning of three foxes, and the foresight of a grand master in chess. To accomplish that, he needed to clear his head, to flush away all distraction, especially the memory of the butterscotch Krimpets, which had already hooked him.

In exactly fifteen minutes, he woke up and started back in.

Like some fairytale tailor, he threaded the end through the maze, dipping and doodling through openings the way he squiggled a football through a defense. As the long August afternoon boiled along, the exploded knot-hairball would cave in here, cave in there. It got lumpy, out of shape, saggy. The *Times* photographer made starbursts with his camera. The people munched on Cobble's pizza and spilled across Hector from sidewalk to sidewalk and said "Ouuuu!" and Ahhhh!"

And then, around dinnertime, a huge roar went up, a volcano of cheers. Cobble's Knot was dead. Undone. Gone. It was nothing but string.

21

*B*ugles, cap guns, sirens, firecrackers, war whoops . . . Cobble's Corner was a madhouse.

Traffic had to beep and inch through the mob. Kids cried for autographs. Scraps of paper fluttered down in a shower of homemade confetti.

A beaming Mr. Cobble handed up a certificate to Maniac for the year's worth of large pizzas. Maniac accepted it and said his thanks. The undone knot lay in a coiled heap at Maniac's feet. Mr. Cobble grabbed it. Already people were guessing how long it was.*

The yelling went on and on, the way yelling does if only to hear itself. But one person wasn't yelling: Amanda Beale. She was holding one of the homemade confetti scraps, gaping at it. Then she was scrambling across the sidewalk, the street, shoving people's legs

---

*It turned out to be four and a half blocks long. Someone tied it to a stop sign and started walking, and that's how far he got before it gave out.

aside, grabbing more scraps, crying out, "Oh no! . . . Oh *no!*" And then she was running.

Maniac saw. He leaped from the table. He picked up a scrap. There was printing on it, about Africa. He picked up another; this one mentioned ants. Another: Aristotle.

The encyclopedia A!

He followed the scrap-paper trail up Hector and down Sycamore, all the way to the Beales' front steps. The only thing left of the book was the blue-and-red cover. It looked something like an empty looseleaf binder. Amanda was hunched over, rocking, squeezing it to her chest. "It was my fault," she sobbed. "I got careless. I left it in the living room. Anybody could look through the window and . . . and . . ." She clenched her eyes so tightly it was a wonder the tears got out.

More than anything, Maniac wanted to hug Amanda and tell her it was okay. He wanted to go inside, be with his family, in his house, his room, behind his window. But that wasn't the right thing. The right thing was to make sure the Beales didn't get hurt anymore. He couldn't keep letting them pay such a price for him.

He turned and headed back up Sycamore. Maybe the man with the can-of-worms voice was right: "Back to your own kind . . . back to your own kind . . ."

He never got farther west than the far curb of Hector Street, because McNab and the Cobras were there to meet him, grinning, leering, hissing, "Yo, baby, we hear ya got a little pizza prize there . . . come on back . . . we missed ya . . . we been waitin' for ya . . ."

So he turned and started walking north on Hector, right down the middle of the street, right down the invisible chalk line that divided East End from West End. Cars beeped at him, drivers hollered, but he never flinched. The Cobras kept right along with him on their side of the street. So did a bunch of East Enders on their side. One of them was Mars Bar. Both sides were calling for him to come over. And then they were calling at each other, then yelling, then cursing. But nobody stepped off a curb, everybody kept moving north, an ugly, snarling black-and-white escort for the kid in the middle.

And that's how it went. Between the curbs, smack-dab down the center, Maniac Magee walked — not ran — right on out of town.

PART II

22

*I*f you were the baby buffalo at the Elmwood Park Zoo, maybe it would have gone something like this:

You wake up. You have breakfast, compliments of mother's milk. You mosey on over to the lean-to. Surprise! A strange new animal in there. Bigger than you, but a lot smaller than Mom. Hair, but only on top of its head. Sitting in the straw, munching on a carrot, like Mom does.

Every morning, same thing. You get to expect it. Some mornings, you forget Mom's milk and head right on over to the lean-to. The creature offers you a carrot, but all you know how to deal with is milk. You nuzzle the new, funny-smelling, hairy-headed animal. It nuzzles you back. Mom doesn't seem to mind.

After the nuzzling, the stranger climbs over the fence and goes away, not to return until that night. Only, one morning the stranger falls from the fence and lies on the ground, on the other side. It doesn't move. You try to poke your nose through the chain links, but you can't reach, you can only watch . . . only watch . . .

The old man was bumping through the zoo in the park pickup when he spotted the body clumped outside the buffalo pen. He wheeled over, got out. "A kid!" At first he could only stare, at the body, then at the baby bison, whose large brown eye seemed to be watching them both. The mother came lumbering over, nodding, as if to confirm: "A kid."

The kid looked terrible. His clothes were scraps, rags. Wherever his body showed through, it was bony and dirty and scratched. The two bison, staring, staring, seemed to say, "Well, *do* something."

The old man gathered his own bones and muscles as best he could and managed to hoist the kid and get him into the pickup. He laid him on the seat, bent his legs so he could close the door.

He knew he should take the kid straight to the hospital, or a doctor, someplace official, someplace right. But the pickup just sort of steered itself back to the band shell, and there he was, lugging the kid into the baseball-equipment room.

The season was over by now, but the army-green burlap bags still stood ready for the next ump to call, "Play ball!" He yanked out a couple of chest protectors and laid the kid down, careful with his head. At least he was breathing.

Though it wasn't cold, it seemed as if the kid ought to be covered, so the old man took his winter work jacket off the hook and laid that over him. Then he waited and watched. With trembling, dusty fingers, he touched the kid's limp, scrawny hand. He had never held, never really touched a kid's hand before . . .

"Hey."

The kid's voice was barely a squeak, but it threw him back. He dropped the hand.

"Where am I?"

The old man cleared his throat. "The band shell."

"The band shell?"

"In the back. Equipment room."

The kid's eyes squinted, blinked. "And you?"

"What about me?"

"Who are you?"

"Grayson."

"Grayson. Do I know you?"

He got up. "Guess you do now." He went to his hot plate, heated up some water, and made some chicken noodle Cup-a-Soup. He gave it to the kid, who was sitting up now. "You want a spoon?"

He looked as though he could hardly lift the cup. He held it with both hands and gulped it down. "Huh?" he said.

"Never mind. You still hungry?"

The kid flopped back down. "A little."

"Wait here," said Grayson, and left.

Ten minutes later he was back with a zep, a large. It took the kid less time to polish it off than it had taken Grayson to get it. He told the kid not to eat so fast, he'd get sick. The kid nodded.

Grayson said, "Where'd you get them scratches?"

"Oh, some picker bush."

"What were you doing there?"

"Hiding."

"Hiding? Who from?"

"Some kids."

"Where?"

The kid pointed. "Somewhere out there. Some other town." He crossed his legs Indian-style on the chest protector. "Can I ask you a favor?"

"Shoot."

"Can we go somewhere and get some butterscotch Krimpets?"

Grayson squawked, "Krimpets! You *still* hungry?"

"For them, I am."

Grayson threw the greasy zep wrapper into the wastebasket. "I don't know. Maybe you oughta do something for me first."

"Like what?"

"Like tell me your name."

"It's Jeffrey Magee."

"And where you live."

"Well, I did live on Sycamore Street. Seven twenty-eight."

"Did?"

"I guess I don't anymore."

The old man stared. "You said Sycamore?"

"Yep."

"Ain't that the East End?"

"Yep."

With his fingernail, he scraped a path of dirt off the kid's forearm. He stared at it.

"What are you doing?" the kid asked.

"Seein' if you was white under there."

Neither spoke for awhile.

At last the kid said, "Anything else you want to ask me?"

The old man shrugged. "Guess not."

"Ah, come on. Don't stop asking."

"I'm asked out."

"How about the zoo, huh? Don't you want to know what I was doing at the zoo? At the buffalo pen?"

The old man sighed. "Okay, what?"

"I was living there."

"With the buffaloes?"

"Yep, with the buffaloes."

"You like buffaloes?"

"It was dark when I got there. I thought it was the deer pen."

"They switched the deer and the buffaloes around last month."

"Okay with me. I got along better with the buffaloes anyway."

"Well, I'll tell you one thing." The old man sniffed. "You sure do smell like one."

The kid laughed. They both laughed. When they finally calmed down, the kid said, "Any chance of those Krimpets now?"

Grayson reached for the pickup keys. "Let's go."

23

Grayson got the Krimpets all right. He bought a whole box of three-packs. With ten packs to a box, that was thirty butterscotch Krimpets. Maniac thought he must have climbed out of that buffalo pen right into Heaven.

Then Grayson took Maniac home. Home for the old man was the Two Mills YMCA. He lived in a room on the third floor. But he didn't take Maniac up there. He took him downstairs to the locker room. He got him a towel and a cake of soap, told him to take off his rags, and pointed the way to the showers.

Maniac stayed in the shower for an hour. He hadn't done this since his last bath with the little ones. He smiled at the thought of them shrieking and splashing. The shower needles stung his scratches, but it was a good, welcome-back-to-town stinging.

When Maniac finally forced himself from the shower, he found the old man waiting with clothes. Grayson's clothes. "I called the U.S. Army in to haul them buffalo rags away," he said. "They come in with gas masks on, and they used tongs to pick 'em up and put 'em in a steel box, and they took the box away to bury it at the bottom of the first mine shaft they come to."

Maniac couldn't stop laughing. Neither could Grayson, especially when he got a load of the kid drowning in his clothes.

An hour later, after a minor shopping spree, Maniac had clothes of his own.

For the rest of the afternoon, they cruised around town, talking and eating Krimpets.

"So," said the old man, "now what're you gonna do?"

Maniac thought it over. "How about a job? I could work for the park, like you."

Grayson didn't answer that. He said, "Where you think you're gonna stay?"

Maniac's answer was prompt: "The baseball room. It's perfect."

A tiny idea was beginning to worm its way into Grayson's head; he could barely feel it as it brushed by all the claptrap in his brain. He ignored it. He said, "What about school?"

Maniac was silent. Some butterscotch icing had stayed behind on a wrapper. He scooped it up and mopped it from his finger, wishing it were Mrs. Beale's, and not his own.

Grayson, who was not comfortable asking questions, was even less comfortable waiting for answers. "I said, what about school?"

Maniac turned to him. "What about it?"

"You gotta go. You're a kid. Ain't ya?"

"I'm not going."

"But you gotta. Doncha? They'll make ya."

"Not if they don't find me."

The old man just looked at him for a while with a mixture of puzzlement and recognition, as though the fish he had landed might be the same one he had thrown away long before. "Why?" he said.

Maniac felt why more than he knew why. It had to do with homes and families and schools, and how a school seems sort of like a big home, but only a day home, because then it empties out; and you can't stay there at night because it's not really a home, and you could never use it as your address, because an address is where you stay at night, where you walk right in the front door without knocking, where everybody talks to each other and uses the same toaster. So all the other kids would be heading for their homes, their night homes, each of them, hundreds, flocking from school like birds from a tree, scattering across town, each breaking off to his or her own place, each knowing exactly where to land. School. Home. No, he was not going to have one without the other.

"If you try to make me," he said, "I'll just start running."

Grayson said nothing. What the kid said actually made him feel good, though he had no idea why. And the brushing little worm of a notion was beginning to tickle him now. He kept on driving.

24

*T*hey got back to the band shell just as they finished the last of the Krimpets. Grayson looked at his watch. "Guess it's time to quit the job I never did today. Time for dinner, too."

Grayson was joking, but Maniac was serious when he piped, "Great! Where to?"

Dumbfounded, the old man drove back out of the park to the nearest diner, where he sat with a cup of coffee while the boy wolfed down meatloaf and gravy, mashed potatoes, zucchini, salad, and coconut custard pie.

Grayson had a way of jumping into a subject without warning; it was during Maniac's dessert that he abruptly said, "Them black people, they eat mashed potatoes, too?"

Maniac thought he was kidding, then realized he wasn't. "Sure. Mrs. Beale used to have potatoes a lot, mashed and every other way."

"Mrs. who?"

"Mrs. Beale. Do you know the Beales? Of seven twenty-eight Sycamore Street?"

The old man shook his head.

"Well, they were my family. I had a mother and father and a little brother and sister and a sister my age and a dog. My own room, too."

Grayson stared out the diner window, as if digesting this information. "How 'bout meatloaf?"

"Huh?"

"They eat that, too?"

"Sure, meatloaf too. *And* peas. *And* corn. You name it."

"Cake?"

Maniac beamed. "Oh, man! You kidding? Mrs. Beale makes the best cakes in the world."

Grayson's eyes narrowed. "Toothbrushes? They use them?"

Maniac fought not to smile. "Absolutely. We all had our toothbrushes hanging in the bathroom."

"I know that," said Grayson, impatient, "but is theirs the same? As ours?"

"No difference that I could see."

"You didn't drink out the same glass."

"Absolutely, we did."

This information seemed to shock the old man.

Maniac laid down his fork. "Grayson, they're just regular people, like us."

"I was never in a house of theirs."

"Well, I'm telling you, it's the same. There's bathtubs and refrigerators and rugs and TVs and beds . . ."

Grayson was wagging his head. "Ain't that some-thin' . . . ain't that somethin' . . ."

It was after dark when they got back to the baseball-equipment room. The worm in Grayson's head had long since ceased to be a tiny tickle; it was now a maddening itch. As with all such itch-worms, it would exit by only one route, the mouth. He said: "Uh, I was thinkin', uh, maybe you want to come over to my place. This here floor's pretty hard." He tapped his foot to show how hard.

The grizzled, gray old parkhand could never know how much Maniac was tempted, or how deeply the offer touched him. Neither could Maniac explain that the bad luck he always seemed to have with parents had led him to the conclusion that he'd better stick to himself.

"Oh, it's not so bad here," he said. "Look — " He lay down on the chest protectors and closed his eyes. "Ah . . . just like a mattress. I can feel myself dozing off already." And then, not wanting to hurt the old man's feelings, he quickly added, "Hey, I told you everything about me. How about you?" He pulled Grayson's coat over himself. "A bedtime story."

Grayson snorted. "Story? I don't know no stories."

"Sure you do," Maniac prodded. "About yourself. You know about you. Everybody has a story."

"Not me." Grayson was edging for the door. "I ain't got no story. I ain't nobody. I work at the park."

"You line baseball fields?"

"Yep. I do that."

"You live at the Y. You drive the park pickup. You like butterscotch Krimpets."

Grayson shook his head. "Not as much as you. I was just eating 'em to be friendly, so's you wouldn't have to eat 'em all by yourself."

"And there's another thing about you." Maniac joked. "You're a liar."

They both laughed.

Grayson opened the door.

"Wait —" called Maniac. "What did you want to grow up to be when you were a kid?"

Grayson paused in the doorway. He looked out into the night. "A baseball player," he said. He turned out the light and closed the door.

25

*I*n the morning Grayson bought Maniac an Egg McMuffin and a large orange juice. He bought the same thing for himself, so they ate breakfast together in the baseball-equipment room.

"You sent me to bed without a story last night," Maniac kidded.

Grayson brushed a yellow speck of egg from his white stubble. "I don't got no stories. I told you."

"You wanted to be a baseball player."

"That ain't no story."

"Well, did you become one?"

Grayson drank half his orange juice. "Just the Minors," he muttered.

Maniac yelped, "The *Minors!*"

"Couldn't never make it to the Majors." There was a frayed weariness in the old man's words, as though they had long since worn out.

"Grayson — the *Minors*. Man, you must have been *good*. What position did you play?"

Grayson said, "Pitcher." This word, unlike the others, was not worn at all, but fresh and robust. It startled Maniac. It declared: I am not what you see. I am not a line-laying, pickup-driving, live-at-the-Y, bean-brained parkhand. I am not rickety, whiskered worm chow. *I am a pitcher.*

Maniac had sensed there was something more to the old man; now he knew what it was. "Grayson, what's your first name?"

The old man fidgeted. "Earl. But call me Grayson, like ever'body." He looked at the clock on the wall. "Gotta go."

"Grayson, wait —"

"I'm late for work. You oughta be in school."

He was gone.

Grayson returned at noon, bearing zeps and sodas, and was not allowed to leave until he told Maniac one story about the Minor Leagues.

So he told the kid about his first day in the Minors, with Bluefield, West Virginia, in the Appalachian League. Class D. "Can't get no lower'n that," he told the kid. "That's where you broke in. Don't have D ball no more."

He told about thumbing a ride to Bluefield, and, when he got there, going up to a gas station attendant and asking which way to the ballpark. And the gas station man told him, "Sure, but first I gotta ask you something. You're a new ballplayer, right? Just comin' on board?" And Grayson said, "Yep, that's right." And the man said, "I thought so. Well then, you're just gonna want to make your first stop right over there" —

he pointed across the street — "that there restaurant, the Blue Star. You just go right on in there and sit yourself down and tell the waitress you want the biggest steak on the menu. And anything else you want, too, because it's all on the house. The Blue Star treats every new rookie to his first meal in town free." He gave a wink. "They want your business."

Great, thought Grayson, and he did just that. Only when he got up and left, the restaurant owner came running after him down the street, all mad at Grayson for skipping out. And when Grayson told him he was a rookie just picking up his free first meal, the owner got even madder. Seems the gas station man was a real card and liked to welcome dumb rookies with his little practical joke.

And that's how it came to be that when the Bluefield Bullets took the field that day, they did so without the services of their new pitcher, who was back in the kitchen of the Blue Star restaurant, doing dishes to work off a sixteen-ounce steak, half a broiled chicken, and two pieces of rhubarb pie.

After a story like that, Maniac couldn't just stay behind, so he tagged along when Grayson went back to work. He helped the old man raise a new fence around the children's petting farmyard. When the park Superintendent came around and asked about the kid, Grayson said it was his nephew come to visit for a while. The Superintendent, who managed the budget, said, "We can't pay him, you know." And Grayson said, "Fine, no problem," and that was that.

From then on Maniac was on the job with Grayson every afternoon. They raised fences, mended fences, hauled stone, patched asphalt, painted, trimmed trees. They ate breakfast, lunch, and dinner together, sometimes in the equipment room, sometimes at a restaurant. They spent weekends together.

All the while Grayson told baseball stories (insisting, all along, "I ain't got no stories"). He told about the Appalachian League and the Carolina League and the Pecos Valley League and the Buckeye and the Mexican Leagues. About the Pedukah Twin Oaks and the Natchez Pelicans and the Jesup Georgia Browns and the Laredo Lariats. All Minor League teams, Minor League baseball.

Sleazy hotels. Sleazy buses. Sleazy stadiums. Sleazy fans. Sleazy water buckets. Curveballs and bus fumes and dreams, dreams of the Majors — clean sheets and an umpire at every base.

Funny stories. Happy stories. Sad stories. Just plain baseball stories.

The happiest story being the one about Willie Mays's very last at-bat in the Minor Leagues, before he went up to the New York Giants and immortality. Well, it was ol' Grayson himself who had last crack at Mays, in the ninth inning of a game with Indianapolis — and what did Grayson do? All he did was set the Say Hey Kid down swinging — on three straight curveballs.

The saddest story was the one about the scout who came down from the Toledo Mud Hens. The Mud Hens had a roster slot, and the scout had a notion to fill it with the pitcher with the wicked curveball, name of Earl Grayson. This was Grayson's big chance, for the Mud Hens were Class AAA ball, one short step from the Majors.

The night before the game, Grayson spent half of it on his knees by his bed, praying. And even five minutes before the game, in the dugout, he bent down, pretending to tie his shoe, and closed one eye and prayed: "Please let me win this ball game." Which was something, since he had never gone to a church in his life. ("God musta fainted," he said to Maniac.)

And indeed, maybe God did, or maybe He only listened to Major Leaguers, because Grayson took the mound and proceeded to pitch the flat-out awfulest game of his life. His curveball wasn't curving, his sinker wasn't sinking, his knuckler wasn't knuckling. The batters were teeing off as if it were the invasion of Normandy Beach. Before the third inning was over, the score was 12–0, and Grayson was in the showers.

He was twenty-seven years old then, and that was the closest he would ever get to the Big Show. He hung on for thirteen more years, a baseball junkie, winding up in some hot tamale league in Guanajuato, Mexico, until his curveball could no longer bend around so much as a chili pepper and his fastball was slower than a senorita's answer.

He was forty, out of baseball, and, for all intents and purposes, out of life. All those years in the game, and all he was fit to do was clean a restroom or sweep a floor or lay a chalk line — or, far, far down the road, tell stories to a wide-eyed, homeless kid.

26

*I*t was impossible to listen to such stories empty-handed. As soon as Grayson started one, Maniac would reach into one of the equipment bags and pull out a ball or a bat or a catcher's mitt. Sniffing the scuffed horsehide aroma of the ball, rippling the fingertips over the red stitching — it's hard to say how these things can make the listening better, but they do, and, for Maniac, they did.

And of course, as happens with baseball, one thing led to another, and pretty soon the two of them were tossing a ball back and forth. And then they were outside, where the throws could be longer; where you could play pepper on the outfield grass of the Legion field, the old man pitching, the kid tapping grounders; where you could shag fungoes, the old man popping high fliers, the kid chasing them down.

And now the stories were mixed with instruction: the grizzled, rickety coot showing the kid how to spray liners to the opposite field; how to get a jump on a long fly even before the batter hits it; how to throw the curveball. Stiff, crooked fingers that grappled clumsily with Krimpet wrappers curled naturally around the shape of a baseball. With a ball in his hand, the park handyman became a professor.

As to the art of pitching, of course, the old man could show and tell, but he could no longer do. Except for one pitch, the only one left in his repertoire from the old days. He called it the "stopball," and it nearly drove Maniac goofy.

The old man claimed he'd discovered the stopball one day down in the Texas League and that he was long gone from baseball when he perfected it. Unlike most pitches, the stopball involved no element of surprise. On the contrary, the old man would always announce it.

"Okay," he'd call in from the mound, "here she comes. Now keep your eye on her, 'cause she's gonna float on up there, and just about the time she's over the plate, she's gonna *stop*. Now, nobody else ever hit it, so don't you go gettin' upset if you don't neither. It's no shame to whiff on the stopball." And then he'd throw it.

Well, of course, Maniac knew that most if not all of that was blarney, and, just to make sure, he watched the ball extra carefully. There sure didn't seem to be anything unusual about it, not at first, anyway; but as the ball came closer, it did somehow seem to get more and more peculiar; and by the time it reached the plate, it might just as well have stopped, because Maniac never knew if he was swinging at the old man's pitch or at his speech. Whatever, in weeks of trying, he never hit out of the infield.

It was October. The trees rimming the outfield were flaunting their colors. The kid and the geezer base-balled their lunchtimes away, and the after-dinner-times and weekends.

And every night, as the old man left for his room at the Y, he would grouse, "You oughta go to school." And one night, the kid said back, "I do."

And that's how the old man found out what the kid was doing with his mornings.

He had noticed the books before, rows and piles of them that kept growing; but their being books, he didn't think much of it. Now, the kid tells him, "You know the money you give me" — each morning he gave the kid fifty cents or a dollar to get himself some Krimpets — "well, I take it up to the library. Right inside the door they have these books they're selling, cases of them, old books they don't want anymore. They only cost five or ten cents apiece." He pointed to the piles. "I buy them."

He showed them to the old man. Ancient, back-broken math books, flaking travel books, warped spellers, mangled mysteries, biographies, music books, astronomy books, cookbooks.

"What's the matter?" said the old man. "Can't you make up your mind what kind you want?"

The kid laughed. "I want them all." He threw his hands out. "I'm learning everything!"

He opened one of the books. "Look . . . geometry . . . triangles . . . okay, isosceles triangles. These two legs, they look equal to you?"

The old man squinted. He nodded.

"Okay, but can you *prove* it?"

The old man studied the triangle for a full minute. "If I had a ruler maybe —"

"No ruler."

The old man sighed. "Guess I give up."

So the kid proved it — absolutely, dead-center proved it.

Two days later, while playing pepper in the Legion infield, the old man said to the kid, "So why don't you go ahead and teach me how to read?"

27

*T*he story he told now was not about baseball. It was about parents who were drunk a lot and always leaving him on his own; about being put in classes where they just cut paper and played games all day; about a teacher who whispered to a principal, just outside the classroom door, "This bunch will never learn to read a stop sign." Right then and there, as if to make the teacher right, he stopped trying.

"The part I didn't tell about Bluefield, I was only fifteen. I ran away."

The kid and the old man climbed into the pickup. They made three stops. First, they stopped by the park office at the zoo, where Grayson told the Superintendent he just wanted to work part-time for a while, in the afternoons. Fine, said the Superintendent, just so you don't expect to get paid full-time.

Then they went to the library book-sale racks and bought about twenty old picture books, such as *The Story of Babar* and *Mike Mulligan's Steam Shovel* and *The Little Engine That Could.*

Then they went to Woolworth's for a small portable blackboard and a piece of chalk.

Within three days, Grayson had the alphabet down pat. The shapes, the sounds.

After a week, he could read ten one-syllable words. But he was reading them from memory. It took another couple of weeks before he began to get the hang of sounding out words he had never seen before.

The old man showed an early knack for consonants. Sometimes he got *m* and *n* mixed up, but the only one that gave him trouble day in and day out was *c*. It reminded him of a bronc some cowboy dared him to ride in his Texas League days. He would saddle up that *c*, climb aboard and grip the pommel for dear life, and ol' *c*, more often than not, it would throw him. Whenever that happened, he'd just climb right back on and ride 'er some more. Pretty soon *c* saw who was boss and gave up the fight. But even at their orneriest, consonants were fun.

Vowels were something else. He didn't like them, and they didn't like him. There were only five of them, but they seemed to be everywhere. Why, you could go through twenty words without bumping into some of the shyer consonants, but it seemed as if you couldn't tiptoe past a syllable without waking up a vowel. Consonants, you knew pretty much where they stood, but you could never trust a vowel. To the old pitcher, they were like his own best knuckleball come back to haunt him. In, out, up, down — not even the pitcher, much much less the batter, knew which way it would break. He kept swinging and missing.

But the kid was a good manager, and tough. He would never let him slink back to the showers, but kept sending him back up to the plate. The kid used different words, but in his ears the old Minor Leaguer heard: "Keep your eye on it . . . Hold your swing . . . Watch it all the way in . . . Don't be anxious . . . Just make contact."

And soon enough, that's what he was doing, nailing those vowels on the button, riding them from consonant to consonant, syllable to syllable, word to word.

One day the kid wrote on the blackboard:

I see the ball.

And the old man studied it awhile and said, slowly, gingerly: "I . . . see . . . the . . . ball."

Maniac whooped, "You're reading!"

"I'm reading!" yipped the old man. His smile was so wide he'd have had to break it into sections to fit it through a doorway.

28

*T*he first book Grayson read cover to cover was *The Little Engine That Could*. It took almost an hour and was the climax to a long evening of effort. At the end, the old man was sweating and exhausted.

The kid's reaction surprised him. He didn't jump and yippee like he did after the first sentence. He just stayed in the far corner, seated on a stuffed and lumpy equipment bag. He had kept his distance all during the reading, letting Grayson know there would be no cheating, he had to do it on his own. Now he was just staring at Grayson, a small smile coming over his face. And now he was making a fist and clenching it toward Grayson, and he said, "A-*men*."

"What's that?"

"A-*men*."

"What's that for? Who prayed?"

"I learned it in the church I used to go to. You don't have to wait for a prayer. You say it when somebody says something or does something you really like." He hopped off the bag, thrust both hands to the ceiling, and shouted: "Aaaay-*men!*"

And suddenly the kid was hugging him, squeezing with a power you never suspected was in that little body, unless you had seen him pole a baseball almost to the trees in dead center field.

"Okay," said Maniac, clapping his hands, "what'll it be? I'll be the cook. Whatever you want."

Maniac had a toaster oven now, compliments of his whiskered friend. In fact, little by little, Grayson had brought him a lot of things: a chest of drawers for his clothes, a space heater, a two-foot refrigerator, hundreds of paper dishes and plastic utensils, blankets, a mat to sleep on (which the kid ignored, preferring the chest protectors). In time the place was homier than his own room at the Y.

"How 'bout a corn muffin?" said Grayson, choosing something easy on his bad teeth and aching gums.

Maniac went to the bookcase that served as a pantry. "One corn muffin coming up. Toasted?"

"Yeah, why not."

"Butter?"

"Sure, butter."

"Something to drink with that, sir?"

"Nah, muffin's enough."

"The apple juice is excellent, sir. It was a great year for apples."

Live it up, thought Grayson. "Yeah, okay, apple juice."

"Coming right up, sir."

After the snack, the kid proved himself as good a

mind reader as a cook. "Why don't you stay over-night?" he said. "It's late."

While he groused about so preposterous an idea, the kid laid down the mat he never used, bulldogged him down to it, pulled off his shoes and draped a blanket over him. He protested, "This is s'pposed to be yours."

The kid patted his chest protectors — "I'm okay . . . I'm okay" — and he knew that was the truth of it.

The old man gave himself up willingly to his exhaustion and drifted off like a lazy, sky-high fly ball. Something deep in his heart, unmeasured by his own consciousness, soared unburdened for the first time in thirty-seven years, since the time he had so disgraced himself before the Mud Hens' scout and named himself thereafter a failure. The blanket was there, but it was the boy's embrace that covered and warmed him. *When somebody does something you really like.* "A-*men*," the old man whispered into the corn-meal- and baseball-scented darkness.

29

*F*or most of November, winter toyed with Two Mills, whispered in its ear, tickled it under the chin. On Thanksgiving Thursday, winter kicked it in the stomach.

But that didn't stop the old man and the boy from joining the ten thousand who thronged to the stadium on the boulevard to see the traditional high school football game. The arctic air laid panes of ice over the crayfish edgepools of Stony Creek. The effect was the opposite on human noses. Maniac's and Grayson's ran like faucets, and not a handkerchief in sight. They deputized their sleeves and grabbed handfuls of napkins from the refreshment stand.

Two Mills won the game, thanks to a last-minute 73-yard TD pass from quarterback Denehy to James "Hands" Down. From the instant his old trash-talking sandlot pal cradled the ball in his long brown fingers, Maniac was jumping on his seat, screaming trash at Hands's pursuers every step to the goal line (and glancing about to make sure Mrs. Beale wasn't hearing).

By the time they got back to the baseball room, they were nearly frozen. But the freeze was good, for it made the warmth of the little apartment all the more welcome. Within fifteen minutes the space heater had the place positively tropical, while in the toaster oven their five-pound Thanksgiving chicken was already beginning to brown. A pair of hot plates and a squad of pots were pressed into action, and by midafternoon the two were sitting down to a feast of roast chicken, gravy, cranberry sauce, applesauce, SpaghettiOs, raisins, pumpkin pie, and butterscotch Krimpets.

Maniac thought of Thanksgivings past, of sitting around a joyless table, his aunt and uncle as silent and lifeless as the mammoth bird they gnawed on. He said this grace: "Dear God, we want to take this opportunity to thank you for the best Thanksgiving dinner we ever had . . . well, *I* ever had. I guess I shouldn't speak for my friend Grayson —" he peeked across the table. "Grayson," he whispered, "is this your best one, too?"

The old man opened one eye; he shrugged. "Don't know. Ain't tasted it yet."

Maniac glared, rolled his eyes upward, hissed: "*Gray*-son."

The old man flinched. "Uh, yeah" — he squinted one-eyed at the chicken — "yeah, I guess it is."

"The best," Maniac prompted.

"The best."

Maniac went on: "And we want to thank you for

this warm house and for our own little family here and for Grayson learning to read. He's already read thirteen books, as I'm sure you already know. And one more thing. If you could find some way to let the Beale family know I'm wishing them a happy Thanksgiving, I'd really appreciate it. They're the ones on seven twenty-eight Sycamore Street, in case there's any other Beales around. Amen."

"Amen," said Grayson.

They stuffed themselves silly, then collapsed and listened to polka music. Grayson had brought over a record player a week before, along with his entire music collection: thirty-one polka records. Grayson loved polkas.

Of course, one cannot listen to polka music for long before getting up and dancing, which is what the two thanksgivers did as soon as their bloated stomachs allowed. They danced and they laughed, record after record. Whether it was the polka that they danced is another question.

It was nearly dark, both of them having re-collapsed, when Maniac said, "Is there any paint around?"

"Guess so," said Grayson. "What for?"

"You'll see. Can you get some, and a brush?"

The old man dragged himself up. "What color?"

"How about black?"

Five minutes later the old man was back. "Got brown. That do?"

"Fine," said Maniac. He opened the can, stirred the paint, put a jacket on, grabbed the brush and went outside. Grayson followed. He watched the kid paint on the outside of the door, in careful strokes:

101

Maniac stepped back, admiring his work. "One oh one," he proclaimed. "One oh one Band Shell Boulevard."

30

*I*f Thanksgiving was wonderful, Christmas was paradise.

By now Grayson had officially moved out of the Y and into 101 Band Shell Boulevard. Thanks to his long acquaintanceship with the locker room attendant, he and Maniac were privileged to continue using the Y's shower facilities at their pleasure.

For decoration outside, they nailed a wreath to the door. There was only one small window, but it had no sill to hold a candle, so some spray snow had to do.

Inside was another story. Santa's elves themselves would have felt at home. Strings of popcorn swooped across the ceiling. Evergreen branches flared at random, dispersing their piney aroma. Wherever there were a few vacant square inches, something Christmassy appeared: a matchbox crèche, a porcelain Santa, a partridge in a pear tree.

One day Grayson dragged a pair of tree limbs in

and started sawing away. When he was finished, a wooden reindeer stood in the room, big enough for Maniac to ride.

Of course, the tree got the most attention of all. By the time the two of them finished trimming it — their tree-trimming instincts having languished for so many Christmases — hardly a pine needle could be seen under the tinsel and balls and whatnot.

In fact, though they were delighted with their effort, the urge to trim was still full upon them. One room was simply too small to hold the spirit bursting. So they went outside and crossed the creek and tramped the woods until they came to a fine and proper evergreen, and there, their footsteps muffled by the carpet of pine needles, their every breath and whispered word arrayed in frosty white, they trimmed their second tree. This time the ornaments were nature's brilliant red-and-yellow necklaces of bittersweet, pungent pinecones, wine-red clusters of sumac berries, abandoned bird-bodied boats of milkweed, delicate thumb-size goblets of Queen Anne's lace.

31

*I*t was still dark when Maniac awoke on Christmas morning. Within an hour or two, the holiday would come bounding down the stairs and squealing 'round the tinseled trees of Two Mills. But for the moment, Christmas bided its time outside, a purer presence.

Maniac shook Grayson awake, but stayed the old man's hand when he reached to turn on the light. They bundled themselves and ventured into the silent night. Maniac carried a paper bag.

Snow had fallen several days before. In much of the town it had been plowed, shoveled, and slushed away; but in the park — along the creek, the woods, the playing fields, the playground — it still lay undisturbed, save for the tracks of rabbits and squirrels. Beyond the tall pines, stars glittered like snowflakes reluctant to fall.

They visited their tree. They stood silently, just to be near it, letting the magic of it drift over them. In the pine-patched moonlight, the Queen Anne's goblets looked for all the world like filigreed silver.

They walked the creek woods all the way to the

zoo, meandering wordlessly throughout the snowy enchantment. As if by design, they both stopped at the same spot, above the half-submerged, rooty clump of a fallen tree. Somewhere under there, they knew, was the den of a family of muskrats. The old man laid a pine branch at the doorway. Maniac whispered: "Merry Christmas."

They visited the animals at the zoo, at least the outdoor ones, wishing them a happy holiday. The ducks seemed particularly pleased to see them.

By the time they came to the buffalo pen, dawn was showing through the trees. Before the old man finished saying, "Wanna boost?" Maniac was up and over the fence. If mother buffalo was glad to see the fence-hopping human again, she didn't show it. But Baby came trotting on over, and the two of them had a warm reunion. Before leaving, Maniac reached into the paper bag and brought out a present. "For you," he said. It was a scarf — or rather, three scarves tied together. He wrapped them around Baby's neck. "Next year I'll get you stockings for your horns," he grinned, "if you have them by then." A final nuzzle, and he was back over the fence.

They headed back home as the town awoke. Breakfast was eggnog and hot tea and cookies and carols and colored lights and love.

As in all happy Christmas homes, the gifts were under the tree. Maniac gave Grayson a pair of gloves and a woolen cap and a book. The book did not appear to be as sturdy as the others lying around. The cover was blue construction paper, and the spine, instead of being bound, was stapled. The text was hand-lettered, and the pictures were stick figures. The title was *The Man Who Struck Out Willie Mays*. The author's name, which Grayson read aloud with some difficulty, was Jeffrey L. Magee.

Maniac, in his turn, opened packages to find a pair of gloves, a box of butterscotch Krimpets, and a spanking, snow-white, never-ever-used baseball.

He was overjoyed. He rushed to the old man and hugged him. The old man put up with that for a second, then pulled away. "Hold on," he said. He went to one of the baseball equipment bags and reached in, tunneled down to the bottom, and came up with another package, this one wrapped crudely in newspaper. "Hiding this'n," he said. "Didn't know if you're the kinda kid sneaks looks."

Maniac tore it open — and gaped helplessly when he saw what it was. To anyone else, it was a ratty old scrap of leather, barely recognizable as a baseball glove, fit for the garbage can. But Maniac knew at once this was Grayson's, the one he had played with all those years in the Minors. It was limp, flat, the pocket long since gone. Slowly, timidly, as though entering a shrine, the boy's fingers crept into it, flexed, curled the cracked leather, brought it back to shape, to life. He laid the new ball in the palm, pressed glove and ball together, and the glove remembered and gave way and made a pocket for the ball.

The boy could not take his eyes off the glove. The old man could not take his eyes off the boy. The record player finished the "Christmas Polka" and clicked off, and for a long time there was silence.

Five days later the old man was dead.

32

*M*ost mornings, Grayson would be the first one out of bed. He would turn on the space heater, visit the band shell lavatory, then heat up some water, get breakfast ready, and finally wake the boy with a gentle shake of the shoulder. On December thirtieth, it was the silence that woke Maniac, and the cold. The space heater wasn't on, no steaming cups sat on the table, the old man was still under the covers.

Maniac went over. "Grayson." He shook the old man. "Grayson?" He took the old man's hand. It was cold.

"Grayson!"

He didn't run to the Superintendent's office. He didn't run to the nearest house. He knew.

He held the cold, limp hand that had thrown the pitch that had struck out Willie Mays, that had betrayed the old man's stoic ways by giving him a squeeze. He began talking to the old man, about places he had been on the road, about places the two of them might have gone to, about everything.

Then he began to read aloud. He read aloud all the books the old man had learned to read, and he finished with the old man's favorite, *Mike Mulligan's Steam Shovel.*

When he looked out the window, it was night. He dragged his chest protectors alongside the old man's mat and lay down, and only then, when he closed his eyes, did he cry.

The funeral, such as it was, took place on the third day of the New Year. Maniac had at last gone to tell someone, the zookeeper, and from then on he pretty much stayed out of the way.

Grayson came to the cemetery in a wooden box. The pallbearers were unknown to Maniac. They were members of the town's trash-collecting corps, and as they huffed and bent to lay the box over the hole, they smelled vaguely of pine and rotten fruit.

Maniac was the only mourner. He had thought the park Superintendent might show. Or the attendant at the Y locker room. Or maybe the lady who ran the park food stand in summer. None was there. Only Maniac and the man from the funeral home and the six pallbearers and two men off to the side, smoking cigarettes and leaning on a little hole-digging tractor that made Maniac think of something. He smiled inwardly: *Hey, Grayson, look — Mike Mulligan's steam shovel had a baby!* High above, a silver plane crossed the sky, silent as a spider.

A voice startled Maniac. "When's he comin'?" It was one of the pallbearers.

The man from the funeral home pushed down the top of his black leather glove to expose his watch. "Should be here now. Should've been here five minutes ago."

"How long we gotta wait?"

The funeral man shrugged. All but one of the pallbearers lit up cigarettes.

Maniac wished he hadn't come. This event had nothing to do with the man who once lived in the body in the wooden box.

"I'm freezing my cochongas off," a pallbearer announced.

"Me, too," said another.

"Hey, y'know" — called one of the gravediggers — "we ain't waitin' all day to fill in that hole."

Everyone looked to the man in the long black coat. He looked again at his watch. "Traffic, probably."

The minister, thought Maniac. *That's who we're waiting for.*

A pallbearer walked over to the funeral man. "We hauled the stiff here, ain't that enough? They only give us an hour."

Another pallbearer chimed in, "Let's go get some doughnuts."

"Hot coffee, baby."

Loud clanks — a gravedigger was striking the baby steam shovel with a spade.

The funeral man sighed. He pulled out his own cigarette, lit it from the glowing tip of the pallbearer's. "Give it two more minutes. Then we'll see."

Maniac waited for one of those minutes, searching the horizon for signs of a minister. Whatever was going to happen at the end of the next minute, he didn't want to see it. So he ran. "Hey, kid!" they called. "Yo, kid!" But he was running . . . running . . .

PART III

PART III

33

January of that year was too cold and dry for snow. It was a month of frozen hardness, of ice.

Maniac drifted from hour to hour, day to day, alone with his memories, a stunned and solitary wanderer. He ate only to keep from starving, warmed his body only enough to keep it from freezing to death, ran only because there was no reason to stop.

Even if the Superintendent had allowed it, he could not have brought himself to stay at the band shell. He returned only long enough to pick up a few things: a blanket, some nonperishable food, the glove, and as many books as he could squeeze into the old black satchel that had hauled Grayson's belongings around the Minor Leagues. Before he left for good, he got some paint and angrily brushed over the 101 on the door.

During the days, he ran, usually a slow jog. But sometimes he would suddenly sprint, furious ten- or twenty-second bursts, as though trying to leave himself behind. Sometimes he walked. He crossed and recrossed the river. He wandered in all directions through all the surrounding communities and townships, Bridgeport, Conshohocken, East Norriton, West Norriton, Jeffersonville, Plymouth, Worcester.

Whenever he crossed the bridge over the Schuylkill, he turned his eyes so as not to see the nearby P & W trestle. Even so, in his mind's eye he saw the red and yellow trolley careening from the high track, plunging to the water, killing his parents over and over. After a while he stopped crossing the bridge.

Other than that, he went wherever there was room to go forward — along roads and alleys and railroad tracks, across fields and cemeteries and golf courses. From high above, a tracing of his routes would have looked as hopelessly tangled as Cobble's Knot.

By nightfall he was back in Two Mills. He would retrieve the satchel from wherever he had stashed it and find a place to endure the night. A few times he revisited the buffalo pen, where he covered himself with a second blanket of straw. Other times his overnight quarters might be an abandoned car, an empty garage, a basement stairwell.

When his original supply of food ran out, he fed himself at the zoo or at the soup kitchen down at the Salvation Army. He did odd jobs for housewives, ran errands for shopkeepers. He would not beg.

One day he found himself among monuments and cannon and rolling hills. He was in Valley Forge. Here the Continental Army had suffered through a winter of their own, and the vast, stark, frozen desolation itself seemed a more proper monument than statues and stones. The only buildings here were tiny log-and-mortar cabins, replicas of the army's shelters. Maniac could feel the ache swelling outward from his breast and filling the enormous, bounding spaces.

He returned to town for the satchel and put himself up in one of the cabins. It was scarcely bigger than a large doghouse. The floor was dirt. There was a doorway, but no door.

Several saltines fell from the blanket. He threw them outside. Let the birds have them. He wrapped himself in the blanket and lay down. He lay there all night and all the next day. Dreams pursued memories, courted and danced and coupled with them and they became one, and the gaunt, beseeching phantoms that called to him had the rag-wrapped feet of Washington's regulars and the faces of his mother and father and Aunt Dot and Uncle Dan and the Beales and Earl Grayson. In that bedeviled army there would be no more recruits. No one else would orphan him.

The second evening came and went. Maniac never stirred. Knowing it would not be fast or easy, and wanting, deserving nothing less, grimly, patiently, he waited for death.

34

*I*t was during the second night in the cabin that he heard the little voices. They were not soldiers' voices.

"I'm goin' in this one."

"No, *that* one. That one's bigger."

"I'm tired. I'm stopping."

"You stupid meatball, it's right *there*. Another two *seconds*."

"I'm stayin'."

"Great, you beef jerky, stay. I'm going to that one. Good-night."

Silence; then: "Hold on! I'm coming!"

That was all. The ghostly soldiers returned, their haunted eyes seeking warmth, food, life.

There was no morning, only daylight in the doorway. He pushed himself up, dragged himself outside into the blinding light. The saltines lay in the brown, frozen grass. The next cabin was nearby.

January slipped an icy finger under his collar and down his back. He pulled the blanket tighter about himself, but it was too late. The finger had touched the last warm coal in his hearth, and his body, fanning the ember, shook itself violently.

He walked to the next cabin, looked inside, and saw a body huddled in the corner. An eye opened, stared at him. Then, in succession, three more eyes opened. The body divided and became two. Two little boys.

"Get a load of this meatball," said the one with a front tooth missing. "He walks around with a blanket on. Hey, meatball, why'nt you bring your mattress along, too?"

"And your pillow, too!" screeched the other.

Then Missing Tooth whipped off his woolen cap and smacked Screecher in the face. Screecher retaliated, and Maniac had to step back while a two-kid tornado swirled around the cabin. When they finished, they rolled onto their backs, shook their legs at the ceiling, and laughed as long as they had fought. The volume coming from Screecher was incredible, as though a microphone were embedded in his throat.

Finally Missing Tooth rediscovered the stranger standing in the doorway. "Hey, meatball, you running away too?"

"No, not really," Maniac replied.

"Well, we are!" went Screecher.

"Where are you going?" Maniac asked.

The answer came from both: "Mexico!"

Maniac bit back a grin. When they stood, he saw

they couldn't have been more than four feet tall or eight years old. "Well," he said, "it's good and warm down there, but it's pretty far, you know."

"Yeah, we know," growled Missing Tooth. "You think we're meatballs like you?" He grabbed a supermarket bag in the corner, opened it. "Look."

It was filled with candy, cupcakes, pies, even a pack of butterscotch Krimpets. Maniac's stomach rasped against itself. He remembered how thirsty he was. "Where'd you get all this?"

"We stold it!" Screecher blurted.

The other smacked him with his cap. "Shut up, Piper, you stupid sausage. You don't go *telling* people you stold stuff."

Piper returned the cap slap. "*You* shut up, Russell. I didn't tell him *where* we stold it."

This time the fight was over in less than a minute. But it started up again when Maniac asked where they were from, and Piper said, "Two Mills," and Russell said, "Shut *up!* He might be a cop!" and bopped him good.

When they settled down, they stared at him warily. Piper snickered. "He ain't no cop. He's a *kid.*"

"Yeah?" sneered Russell. "That's how much *you* know. They got cops that *look* like kids. That's how they *catch* kids."

They stared at him some more. They moved in cautiously, one on either side. They opened his blanket. They patted him all over. "What're we doing this for?" Piper wanted to know.

"We're feelin' for a gun," Russell explained.

"Oh."

After the patting, they backed off. "So," said Russell, "you ain't a cop?"

"Not me," said Maniac. He moved in from the doorway. "I'm" — and with only a moment's pause, the story came to him — "a pizza delivery boy. We have a contest every week, and you two were chosen for a free pizza."

The two gaped at each other. "We *were?*"

"Yep. A large."

"Where is it?" demanded Russell, glancing around.

"At Cobble's Corner. You have twenty-four hours to claim your prize."

He waited while they bickered over what to do. Valley Forge was a good five or six miles from Two Mills. These kids might not have made it to Mexico, but they had come a long way and stayed out overnight, and someone somewhere must be worried sick about them. And he had a feeling they weren't kidding about stealing the food.

He figured he'd better help them make up their minds. "You know," he said, "you're taking the long way to Mexico. If you come back to Two Mills with me, I'll show you a shortcut."

That did it. Soon the three of them were trekking past the Washington Memorial Chapel, Russell and Piper with their bag, Maniac with his satchel.

It was early afternoon when they walked into Cobble's Corner at Hector and Birch. Maniac produced his certificate for conquering Cobble's Knot, and twenty minutes later the young runaways were attacking a large pizza with pepperoni. Maniac confined himself to three glasses of water and half a dozen Krimpets.

The boys agreed with Maniac that they ought to stay the night in their own house before setting out for Mexico in the morning. They were barely a block from Cobble's when Maniac heard a familiar voice. Bellowing and barreling down the street was the fearsome fastballer, king of the Cobras, Big John McNab himself, and he was roaring mad.

Maniac might have taken off, but he found himself clung to and clutched by the two little urchins. They huddled behind him like babies on a possum's back as Giant John came red-faced and huffing up to them. "Where you been?" he yelled.

As Maniac considered what to say, the urchins peeped from behind him: "We wasn't noplace, John. We was right here. With this here kid. And he ain't no cop neither. We checked him out."

For the first time Giant John looked straight at Maniac. A smile crossed his face. "Well, well, the frog man." The smile vanished. "So what're you doing with my little brothers?"

35

*I*t took a while for everything to get straightened out.

First, Giant John had to be convinced that Maniac was not kidnapping his brothers. Then the brothers had to do some more trembling and clinging while John finished lambasting them for running away, which apparently they did about every other week.

Then, when the brothers found out that their pizza person was none other than the famous Maniac Magee, the very same one who had blasted their big brother's fastballs to smithereens and finished him off with a home-run frog, well, it took a good five minutes of rolling on the sidewalk to get all the laughing out of their systems.

Which, of course, got Giant John more than a little steamed.

Prompting Maniac, who didn't like seeing John disgraced before his little brothers, to say, "Yeah, but didn't John tell you what happened the next day?"

And the brothers said, "No, what?"

And Giant John said, "Huh?"

And Maniac winked at John and crossed his fingers. "Sure, John, you remember" — (wink, wink) — "at the Little League field the next day, you said I was lucky that all you threw me was fastballs, because you weren't ready to reveal your secret pitch, the one you'd been working on. Remember?" (Wink.)

McNab nodded dumbly.

"And so I said, 'Well, come on, I can hit anything, pitch it to me.' And you pitched it, and I missed it by a mile, and you kept pitching it to me all day long, and I never even hit a foul ball on it."

"What was the pitch? What was the pitch?" chanted the urchins.

"It was" — Maniac paused for dramatic buildup — "the stopball."

"The *stopball?*"

"Yeah, and you should've seen it. It comes right up to the plate, looking all fat and easy to belt, and then, just when you take your swing" — Maniac got into his batter's stance and demonstrated — "it sort of — *stops* — and your bat just *whiffs* the air." He whiffed at an imaginary stopball.

"Wow," said the brothers, gazing up at their big brother.

And so Maniac was invited to accompany the brothers McNab to their home.

Despite the cold, the front door was wide open, and Maniac could smell the inside before he could see it. The first thing he did see was a yellow, short-haired mongrel looking innocently up at him while taking a leak in the middle of the living room floor.

"Clean that up," John ordered Russell.

"Clean that up," Russell ordered Piper.

Piper just walked on by.

After closing the front door, which was surprisingly heavy, Maniac found a stack of newspapers in a corner. He laid some over the puddle to soak in, then gave himself a tour of the downstairs.

Maniac had seen some amazing things in his lifetime, but nothing as amazing as that house. From the smell of it, he knew this wasn't the first time an animal had relieved itself on the rugless floor. In fact, in another corner he spotted a form of relief that could not be soaked up by newspapers.

Cans and bottles lay all over, along with crusts, peelings, cores, scraps, rinds, wrappers — everything you would normally find in a garbage can. And everywhere there were raisins.

As he walked through the dining room, something — an old tennis ball — hit him on top of the head and bounced away. He looked up — into the laughing faces of Russell and Piper. The hole in the ceiling was so big they both could have jumped through it at once.

He ran a hand along one wall. The peeling paint came off like cornflakes.

Nothing could be worse than the living and dining rooms, yet the kitchen was. A jar of peanut butter had crashed to the floor; someone had gotten a running start, jumped into it, and skied a brown, one-footed track to the stove. On the table were what appeared to be the remains of an autopsy performed upon a large bird, possibly a crow. The refrigerator contained two food groups: mustard and beer. The raisins here were even more abundant. He spotted several of them moving. They weren't raisins; they were roaches.

The front door opened, and seconds later a man clomped into the kitchen. He wore no winter jacket, only a sleeveless green sweatshirt, which ballooned over his enormous stomach. Tattoos blued his upper arms. His hands were nearly pure black. Stale body odor mingled with that of fries and burgers coming from the Burger King bag he held. Dropping the bag next to the bird remains, he bellowed "Chow!" and took a beer from the fridge; he downed a good half of it in one swig, belched, doubled-clutched, and belched again. He had to know someone besides himself was standing in the kitchen, and, just as obviously, he didn't care.

Two floor-quaking crashes came from the dining room — "Geronimo!" . . . "Geronimo!" Russell and Piper had taken the direct route via the hole. "Wha'd ya bring, Dad? Whoppers? Yeah — Whoppers!"

They tore into the bag like jackals into carrion. Plastic flew, fries flew. They both wanted the same Whopper. Mashed between their tugging fists, the Whopper splurted sauce and cheese and pickle chips; then it split. Russell lurched backward into the kitchen table with his half; Piper lurched backward in the opposite direction, and with nothing to stop him, sailed right through the cellar doorway and down the cellar steps. The final thud was followed by the truck-horn blast of Piper's laughter.

When Giant John ambled in, the father said, "Get the blocks?"

"No," grunted John, pulling out a pair of Whoppers. He tossed one to Maniac.

"We need more," growled the father. John didn't answer. "We need *more*."

"I heard."

McNab smashed the tabletop; three fries and a bird wing jumped to the floor. "Now!"

John walked out, nonchalantly munching. "I was busy."

The rest of the night was scenes from a loony movie.

Scene: McNab the father swaggers bare-armed out the front door, bellowing back, "Do yer homework!"

Scene: Maniac retrieves the wet newspaper from the living room. There are no wastebaskets in the house. He finds a trash can in the backyard, next to a pile of cinder blocks. He dumps the soggy papers in the can, which is empty.

Scene: Small turds of an unfamiliar shape appear here and there along the baseboards of the first floor. *Please don't be rats,* Maniac prays.

Scene: The Cobras come in. They glare at Maniac, but Giant John tells them to lay off. They raid the fridge for beer. They smoke cigarettes. They belch and fart. They curse. Russell and Piper, kiddie Cobras, pop their own beer cans, guzzle, swagger, belch, smoke, curse.

Scene: Football game, from the front of the living

room to the back of the dining room. Except for space, it has everything a regular game has — running, passing, blocking, tackling, kicking. There is little furniture to get in the way. Ordinarily, the windows wouldn't last five minutes, but the windows of this house are boarded up with plywood. Body-blocked Cobras fly into the walls. The house flinches.

Scene: A faint rustling noise behind the stove. Oh, no, rats! Maniac dares to look. It's a turtle, box turtle, munching on old Whopper lettuce. Whew!

Scene: The boys' bedroom. Russell and Piper lie prone at the hole. They fire toy submachine guns — tata-tata-tata-tata — at the Cobras heading out the front door. Piper jumps up and blows Maniac away, killing him at least fifteen times. "This is how we're gonna do it! Bam-bam-bam!"

"The guns'll be real," says Russell, still prone and firing, the stock of the toy gun tight against his cheek.

"Yeah!" squawks Piper. "Real!" He flops back to the floor, sprays the whole downstairs. "Soon's they start comin' in — bam-bam-bam!"

"Who?" says Maniac.

"The enemy," says Russell.

"Who's that?" says Maniac.

Russell stops firing long enough to send Maniac a where-have-you-been? look. "Who do ya think?" he sneers. He points the red barrel of the submachine gun toward the bedroom door. Toward the east. The East End.

The heavy front door.

Scene: Darkness. Silence. Sometime early morning.

Maniac lies between the two brothers, on the bed. Do cockroaches climb bedposts? Unable to sleep, asking himself: *What am I doing here?* Remembering: Hester and Lester on his lap, Grayson's hug, corn muffin in the toaster oven. Thinking: *Who's the orphan here, anyway?*

Hearing, as he at last lowers himself into sleep's deep waters, a door slam, a slurred voice: "Do yer homework!"

Fearing: *Will I float?*

36

*T*he deal was, if Russell and Piper went to school for the rest of the week, Maniac would show them the shortcut to Mexico on Saturday. He figured if they all managed to survive till then, he'd come up with something.

On Saturday, the boys had their paper bag packed, and Maniac had a new deal: go to school for another week, and he'd treat them to another large pizza. Besides, he said, crossing his fingers, this was volcano season down in Mexico. The whole place was a sheet of red-hot lava. Better wait till it cools down.

They bought it. And they bought the same deal the following week.

But school was still agony for the boys. It had to be worth more than a pizza a week. But what? The brothers thought and thought about it and soon began to realize that the answer was sleeping between them every night.

Ever since the famous Maniac Magee had showed

up at their house, Russell and Piper McNab had become famous in their own right. Other kids were always crowding around, pelting them with questions. What's he like? What's he say? What's he do? Did he really sit on Finsterwald's front steps? Is he really that fast?

Kids started giving them knots — sneaker laces, yo-yo strings, toys — and saying, "Ask Maniac to undo this, will ya?" Really little kids referred to him as "Mr. Maniac."

The McNabs ate it up. In the streets, the playgrounds, school. The attention, not the pizza, was the real reason they put up with school each day. They began to feel something they had never felt before. They began to feel important.

What a wonderful thing, this importance. Waiting for them the moment they awoke in the morning, pumping them up like basketballs, giving them bounce. And they hadn't even had to steal it! They loved it. The more they had, the more they wanted.

And so, when Maniac tried to cut the next pizza-for-school deal, Russell answered, "No."

"No?" echoed Maniac, who had been afraid it would come to this.

"No," said Russell. "We want something else."

"Oh," said Maniac. "What's that?"

They told him. If he wanted another week's worth of school out of them, he would have to enter Finsterwald's backyard — "and stay there for ten minutes!" screeched Piper, who shuddered at the very thought. When Maniac casually answered, "Okay, it's a deal," Piper ran shrieking from the house.

On the next Saturday morning, Russell, Piper, and Maniac set out for Finsterwald's house, about seven blocks away. They took the alleys. Along the way they were joined by other kids, who were waiting, their eyes at once fearful and excited. By the time they got to Finsterwald's backyard, at least fifteen kids huddled against the garage door on the far side of the alley.

Maniac didn't hesitate. He walked straight up to the back gate, opened it, and went in. Not only that, he went all the way to the center of the yard, turned, folded his arms, smiled, and called "Who's keeping time?"

Russell, his throat too dry to speak, raised his hand.

For ten minutes, fifteen kids — and possibly the universe — held their breath. The only sounds were inside their heads — the moaning and wailing of the ghosts of all the poor slobs who had ever blundered onto Finsterwald's property.

To the utter amazement of all, when Russell finally croaked, "Time," Maniac Magee was still there, alive, smiling, apparently unharmed. Even more amazing, he didn't come out. Instead, he said, "Say, you guys, how about adding to the deal? If I do something else while I'm here, will you make it the next *two* weeks at school?"

"W-watta you g-gonna do?" stammered Russell.

Maniac thought for a minute, then announced brightly, "I'll knock on the front door."

Five kids finsterwallied on the spot. Several others

screamed, "No! Don't!" Piper went into some sort of fit and began kicking the garage door. Russell zoned out.

Maniac took all of this to signify a deal. He hopped the backyard fence and strolled around front.

The others went back down the alley and around the long way. They stationed themselves not only across the street but almost halfway up the block. And even then, they squeezed together in a bunch, as though, if they allowed any space between them, Finsterwald might somehow pick them off, one by one.

They huddled, trembling, to bear witness to the last seconds of Maniac Magee's life. They saw him stand directly in front of the red brick, three-story house, the bile-green window shades. They saw him climb the three cement steps to the white door, the portal of death. They saw him raise his hand, and though they were too far away to hear, they saw him knock upon the door, and fifteen hearts beat in time to that silent knocking.

The door opened. *Finsterwald's door opened.* Not much, but enough so the witnesses could make out a thin strip of blackness. Would Maniac be sucked into that black hole like so much lint into a vacuum cleaner? Would Finsterwald's long, bony hand dart out, quick as a lizard's tongue, and snatch poor Maniac? Maniac appeared to be speaking to the dark crack. Was he pleading for his life? Would his last words be skewered like a marshmallow by Finsterwald's dagger-tipped cane?

Apparently not.

The door closed. Maniac bounded down the steps and came jogging toward them, grinning. Three kids bolted, sure he was a ghost. The others stayed. They invented excuses to touch him, to see if he was still himself, still warm. But they weren't positively certain until later, when they watched him devour a pack of butterscotch Krimpets.

37

*T*hus began a series of heroic feats by Maniac Magee.

At twenty paces, he hit a telephone pole with a stone sixty-one times in a row.

When the once-a-week freight train hit Elm Street, he started running from the Oriole Street dead end — *on one rail* — and beat the train to the park, no-sweat.

He took off his sneaks and socks and walked — nonchalant as you please — through the rat-infested dump at the foot of Rako Hill.

The mysterious hole down by the creek, the one you would never reach into, even if you dropped your most valuable possession into it — he stuck his hand in, his *arm* in, all the way to the elbow, kept it there for the longest sixty seconds on record, and pulled it out, dirty, but still full of fingers.

He climbed the fence at the American bison pen at the zoo — he had suggested this feat himself, everyone else scoffing — and, while the mother looked on, kissed the baby buffalo.*

So it went through February and March of that year, a feat a week.

To much of the town, hearing about these things, it was simply a case of the legend adding to itself, doing what legends do. To Russell and Piper McNab, it was a case of boosting their importance ever higher in the eyes of the other kids. Was it not at the brothers' direction that Maniac Magee performed these deeds? And who after all is the more amazing, the lion or the tamer?

As for Maniac, he understood early on that he was being used for the greater glory of Piper and Russell. He also understood that without him, they would not be going to school every day. For the McNabs, there was nothing free about public education. A tuition had to be paid. Every week Maniac paid it. (And besides, he loved to meet the challenges they cooked up for him.)

And then one day they gave him the most perilous challenge of all. They dared him to go into the East End.

---

*Nobody knows why "buffalo" became "bull" in the jump-rope song. History often gets things wrong.

38

*T*he witnesses — there were twice fifteen this time — went with him as far as Hector Street. They halted at the curb. He crossed the street and went on alone.

Piper megaphoned after him: "Maniac! Come back! We was just kidding! You don't have to!"

Maniac just waved and went on.

He knew he should be feeling afraid of these East Enders, these so-called black people. But he wasn't. It was himself he was afraid of, afraid of any trouble he might cause just by being there.

It was the day of the worms. That first almost-warm, after-the-rainy-night day in April, when you bolt from your house to find yourself in a world of worms. They were as numerous here in the East End as they had been in the West. The sidewalks, the streets. The very places where they didn't belong. Forlorn, marooned on concrete and asphalt, no place to burrow, April's orphans. Once, when he was little in Hollidaysburg, he had gone along with his toy wheelbarrow, carefully lifting them with a borrowed kitchen fork, until the barrow was full, then dumped them into Mr. Snavely's compost pile.

And sure as the worms followed the rain, the kids followed the worms. West End — East End — they had poured from their houses onto the cool, damp sidewalks, and if they gave the worms any notice, it was only when they squashed one underfoot.

And so as Maniac moved through the East End, he felt the presence of not one but two populations, both occupying the same territory, yet each unmindful of the other — one yelping and playing and chasing and laughing, the other lost and silent and dying by the millions . . .

"Yo — fishbelly!"

Maniac snapped to. He glanced at a street sign. He was four blocks from Hector, deep in the East. Mars Bar came dip-jiving toward him, taller than before, bigger, but still scowling. "Hey, fish. Thought you was gone."

Maniac turned to face him fully. Mars Bar did not stop till he was inside Maniac's phone booth of space, inches from his face. They locked eyes, levelly, Maniac thinking, *I must be growing, too*. He said, "I'm back."

The scowl fiercened. "Maybe nobody told you — I'm badder than ever. I'm getting badder every day. I'm almost afraid to wake up in the morning" — he leaned in closer — " 'cause-a how bad I mighta got overnight."

Maniac smiled, nodded. "Yeah, you're bad, Mars."

He gave a sniff; his smile went a little smirky. "And, *I'm* getting so bad myself, I think I must be half black."

Mars's eyes bulged, he backed off, the scowl collapsed, and he howled with laughter. His buddies, who were hanging back, stared dumbly.

As Mars unwound from his laughing fit, he studied Maniac up and down; aware, too, that Maniac was studying him. When he could speak again, he said, "Still them raggedy clothes, huh, fish?" He lifted one foot, posed. "I seen ya looking. Like them kicks? Just got 'em."

Maniac nodded. "Nice."

They were more than nice. They were beautiful. The best — yes, the baddest — sneaks he had ever seen. Way better than anything Grayson could have afforded.

"I forgot to tell you something else, too, fish."

"What's that?"

"I'm fast. I mean, I'm fas-*ter*. I been workin' out. Got my new boss kicks." He sprinted in place, arms and legs pistoning to a blur. He stopped. He jabbed a finger at Maniac's nose, pressed it, flattening the soft end of it. "See — guess you were right — now at least you got a black nose."

He laughed. They both laughed. Everybody laughed. Then Mars turned scowly again, saying, "But you ain't black enough or bad enough to beat the Mars man. We gonna race, honky donkey."

The race was set up on Plum Street, the long, level block between Ash and Jackson. By the time they were ready, half the kids in the East End were there, from the tiniest pipsqueaks to high-schoolers. The little kids ran races of their own from curb to curb. The bigger kids shouldered blasters and dug into their jeans for coins to bet with. For the first time since last fall, mothers opened windows and leaned out from second stories. Traffic was detoured from both ends of the block.

No one could find string for the finish, so a second-story mother dropped down a spool of bright pink thread. Another problem was the start. First, they had to find chalk to draw the starting line. When they did, nobody could seem to draw it straight. The result: a stack of starting lines creeping up the street, till someone brought out a yardstick and did it right.

The next problem came when the starter, Bump Gilliam, who was also Mars Bar's best pal, called, "Get ready!" — and someone in the crowd yelled, "That ain't what you say! You say, 'Take your mark'!"

Well, everybody jumped into it, then. There was shoving and jawing and almost a fistfight over the proper way to start a race. Finally there was a compromise, and Bump called, "Get ready on your mark!" At which point someone else called, "Go, Mars!" and Bump turned and snarled, "Shut up! When the starter starts, there's no noise!" So, naturally, someone else called, "Smoke 'im, Mars!" and then came "Waste 'im, Mars!" and "Do the honk, Bar Man!" And they might still be calling to this day had not a single voice separated itself from the others: "Burn 'im, Magee!" It was Hands Down, laughing and pointing from his perch on the roof of a car.

Bump jumped into the let-up: "Get set! — Go!"

And at long last, mossy from their wait at the starting line, they went.

Even as the race began — even after it began — Maniac wasn't sure how to run it. Naturally he wanted to win, or at least to do his best. All his instincts told him that. But there were other considerations: whom he was racing against, and where, and what the consequences might be if he won.

These were heavy considerations, heavy enough to slow him down — until the hysterical crowd and the sight of Mars Bar's sneaker bottoms and the boiling of his own blood ignited his afterburners, and before you could say, "Burn 'im, Magee!" he was ahead, the pink thread bobbing in his sights. But he never saw his body break the thread; he saw only the face of Mars Bar, straining, gasping, unbelieving, losing.

They went crazy. They went wild. They went totally bananas.

"You *see* him? He turned a-*round!*"

"He ran *backwards!*"

"He did it *backwards!*"

"He beat 'im goin' *backwards!*"

Mars Bar tried. He shoved Bump. "You started too fast! I wasn't ready!" He shoved the thread-holders. "You moved it up so's he could win! I was gaining on 'im!" He shoved Maniac. "You bumped me! You got a false start! You cheated!" But his protests drowned in the pandemonium.

Why did I do it? was all Maniac could think. He hadn't even realized it till he crossed the line, and he regretted it instantly. Wasn't it enough just to win?

Did he have to disgrace his opponent as well? Had he done it deliberately, to pay back Mars Bar for all his nastiness? To show him up and shut him up once and for all? His only recollection was a feeling of sheer, joyful exuberance, himself in celebration: shouting "A-*men!*" in the Bethany Church, bashing John McNab's fastballs out of sight, dancing the polka with Grayson.

Maybe it was that simple. After all, who asks why otters toboggan down mudbanks? But that didn't make it any less stupid or rotten a thing to do. The hatred in Mars Bar's eyes was no longer for a white kid in the East End; it was for Jeffrey Magee, period.

The crowd surged with him as he made his way westward. It wasn't clear whether they were glad or not that he had won, only that they had seen something to set them off. They jostled and jammed and high-fived and jived. For every one who called him "White Lightning," two more challenged him to race, "Right here, baby — you and me — see who gonna turn his back on *who.*"

Maniac kept moving, embarrassed, wishing he could just break out and sprint for the West End, wishing he could duck into the Beales' house and be sanctuaried there and not fear reprisals on them — and just about then, miraculously, two little hands were worming into his, two familiar voices squealing, "Maniac! Maniac!" Hester and Lester! He snatched them up, one in each arm. He was on Sycamore Street. There was the house, the door opening, Amanda, Mrs. Beale smiling to beat the band.

39

*D*uring the night, March doubled back and grabbed April by the scruff of the neck and flung it another week or two down the road. When Maniac slipped silently from the house at dawn — the only way he'd ever manage to get away — March pounced with cold and nasty paws. But Maniac wasn't minding. The reunion had been ecstatic and tearful and nonstop happy, and inside he was pure July. He was half a block up Sycamore before he stopped tiptoeing. Minutes later he crossed Hector. The streets were dry. An occasional scrap of chewed rawhide was all that remained of the worms.

Hours later, Russell and Piper spotted him three blocks off.

"Maniac! You're alive!"

"We thought they got ya! We thought they slit yer throat!"

"We thought they strangled ya and pulled yer tongue out!"

"We thought they chopped yer head off and . . . and . . ."

"And boiled ya!"

"Yeah, boiled ya!"

"And drunk yer blood!"

"Yeah!"

"And drunk yer brains!"

"Ya don't drink brains, ya moron meatball!"

"Yeah, ya do. Brains're like milkshakes. Like Dairy Queen. You can drink 'em with a straw. You can hear 'em sloshin' if you shake yer head hard enough. Listen —"

"Hey — get off my head! Hey! *Help!*"

They were off and running.

Maniac couldn't help laughing. In spite of their twisted, ludicrous impressions of East Enders, the concern and the tears in their eyes had been genuine. They had really missed him. They had really been afraid for him.

Two houses away he could hear the thump — almost feel it — and father George McNab's voice: "Lay 'em down easy, I said. Easy!" Followed by son John: "This easy enough?" *Thump!* Followed by a string of curses from George McNab that fried the cold morning like an egg.

The living room was hazy with dust. At the back end of the dining room, they were bringing in the cinder blocks — George and John and a handful of Cobras — lugging and grunting them in from the backyard and dumping them onto the floor. *Thump! Thump!*

"Hey, kid" — George McNab was pointing through the haze. Three months and he still didn't know his tenant's name. "Get yer lily hide over here. Start luggin' these."

Maniac waved. "Later. Gotta go." He shut the door and headed up the street.

So, they were really doing it. He had heard them planning it for weeks. Making drawings. Buying, or stealing, cement, trowels, a level. "A pillbox," they called it.

Once it was done, they'd be ready. Let the revolt begin. Let the "rebels," as they called the East Enders, come. Let 'em bust through the newly installed bars over the plywood on the windows. Let 'em bust through the steel door. They'll find themselves staring down the barrel of a little surprise. They squabbled over what the surprise should be. Uzi. AK-47. Bazooka.

"Why?" Maniac had asked Giant John one day.

"Why what?"

"Why are you doing all this?"

"To get ready, what else?"

"Well, what do you think's going to happen?"

"What's gonna *happen?*" Giant John swatted a squad of roaches from the kitchen table and sat down. "What's gonna happen is, one of these days they're gonna revolt."

"Who says?"

"Who cares who says? You think they're gonna make an announcement?"

Maniac tried to picture Amanda and Hester and

Lester and Bow Wow storming the barricades. "When's all this supposed to happen?"

John shrugged. "Ya never know. Maybe this summer." He jumped up, grapped a beer from the fridge, flipped it open. "They like to revolt in the summer. Makes 'em itchy. They like to overrun the cities. This time we'll be ready."

And he told Maniac what he often imagined, lying in bed: the blacks sweeping across Hector one steaming summer night; torches, chains, blades, guns, war cries; marauding, looting, overrunning the West End; climbing in through smashed windows, doors, looking for whites, bloodthirsty for whites, like Indians in the old days, Indians on a raid . . .

"That's what they are," Giant John nodded thoughtfully, "today's Indians."

The cockroach strolling up his pant leg wasn't the only thing making Maniac feel crawly. He shook off the roach. He moved to the center of the kitchen, to surround himself with as much space as possible. "But other people," he said, "I don't hear them talking about revolts. Nobody else wants to make a pillbox."

Giant John tilted the last of the beer into his mouth. "Maybe when we do," he grinned, "they will."

That had been weeks before, and now the pillbox was under way, no longer an idea in the backyard but a reality in the dining room. Now there was no room that Maniac could stand in the middle of and feel clean. Now there was something else in that house, and it smelled worse than garbage and turds.

40

*H*e ran far that day, away from the town, letting the wind wash him.

When he returned to the West End, he heard in the distance Mrs. Pickwell whistling her children to dinner. Though he had heard the whistle many times, he had not answered it since his first day in town. Now he felt, as he had that day, that it was meant for him.

This time, of course, there was a difference. He was no stranger. He was Maniac Magee, the kid who had walked barefoot through the dump near their house. The Pickwell kids cheered when he showed up and treated him like a legend in the flesh. Mrs. Pickwell did better: she treated him like a member of the family, as if she would have been surprised if he hadn't come on the whistle. Nor was Maniac the only visitor for dinner. Mr. Pickwell had brought home a down-and-out shoe salesman in sore need of sympathy and a good meal.

As Maniac ate and talked and laughed his way

through dinner, he couldn't help thinking of the Beales. How alike the two families were: friendly, giving, accepting. So easily he could picture the Beales' brown faces around this dinner table, and the little Pickwell kids' white bodies in the bathtub at 728 Sycamore. Whoever had made of Hector Street a barrier, it was surely not these people.

Fortified by his good time at the Pickwells', Maniac returned to the McNabs'. After the East End scare, Russell and Piper no longer demanded stunts of him in return for attending school. On the one hand, this was a relief to Maniac; on the other, it left him with less influence over them.

He could always extort a day or two in class from them with the free weekly pizza. Beyond that, he goaded them toward school any way he could. He organized a marbles tournament that could take place only in the schoolyard during recess. He tried reading to them, as he had to Hester and Lester and to Grayson, but they paid as much attention as the roaches. He took them to the library, then scrapped that idea after their shenanigans left the librarian blubbering and blue-faced.

Then May arrived with its warm weather and blew away what little power he had left. The boys began again to dream of travel. Wood appeared in the backyard. They were building a raft. "Gonna sail down the river to the ocean," they said.

One day he heard frenzied horn-honking and screaming. He turned to see an ancient, rusty, gas-hog convertible rolling by, with Russell behind the wheel and Piper jumping up and down and shrieking in the back seat. By the time Maniac caught up, they were gone and the car was shuddering against a telephone pole.

Another time, he had to run them down and haul them back to Dorsey's Grocery, where he made them empty their bulging pockets of the fifty bubblegums they had stolen.

It was a maddening, chaotic time for Maniac. Running in the mornings and reading in the afternoons gave him just enough stability to endure the zany nights at the McNabs'. When he asked himself why he didn't just drop it, drop them, the answer was never clear. It wasn't so much that he wanted to stay as that he couldn't go. In some vague way, to abandon the McNab boys would be to abandon something in himself. He couldn't shake the suspicion that deep inside Russell and Piper McNab, in the prayer-dark seed of their kidhoods, they were identical to Hester and Lester Beale. But they were spoiling, rotting from the outside in, like a pair of peaches in the sun. Soon, unless he, unless somebody did something, the rot would reach the pit.

And yet he held back. Oh, he prodded and persuaded and inspired and bribed the boys to do right, but he never forced them, never commanded, never shouted. Because to do so would be parental, and he was not yet ready for that. How could he act as a father to these boys when he himself ached to be somebody's son?

* * *

But then one day the boys went too far. He found them playing with the old glove Grayson had given him for Christmas. As if that weren't bad enough, they were using it as a football, punting it back and forth.

Maniac exploded. He popped off for a good ten minutes, got it all out. This was the last straw, he told them. From now on it was gonna be different. No more Mr. Nice Guy. "When I say 'Jump,' you say 'How high?' Got it?"

They got it. For the first time in their lives, the boys were speechless. Speechless as they did their homework that night. Speechless as they went to bed at nine o'clock. Speechless as they went off to school next morning.

The peace lasted three days. Shock accounted for the first day. The second and third days were a new game, called Obedience, or Being Good. When the game lost its appeal, Maniac lost his power. He told them to sit, they stood. He told them to stand, they sat. Instead of going to school, they worked on their raft. Instead of doing homework, they played war in the pillbox. They brought their plastic weapons down from the hole and stationed themselves at the two small gunnery slots in the cinder-block wall and blasted away at anyone moving through the house, not to mention imaginary "rebels" streaming through the door and over the windowsills.

"Stop!" Maniac finally yelled, and snatched the two red gun barrels protruding from the slots. In a moment, two more barrels appeared.

"Stop!" he commanded.

"Ain't shooting you," Russell whined. "We're shooting them rebels. Bam-bam-bam! Pow! Got one! Pow! Bam! Got another! Bam-bam!"

"I said STOP!" Maniac grabbed the guns, threw them on the floor, and stomped on them. He didn't stop till they were plastic splinters.

The only sound was that of the turtle scratching somewhere in the room. The gunnery slots framed the boys' dumbstruck faces.

Russell was the first to speak. "Get outta my house."

"Yeah," sneered Piper, "*outta* here."

Maniac went upstairs, got his satchel, and was gone.

That night and the next night he slept at the park. The following day, as he sat reading in the library, in came the McNab boys. They rushed to him. "Hey, Maniac," blurted Piper, "we been lookin' all over for ya. Ya gotta come to my birthday party. I'm having a party tomorra. Waddaya say, huh? Ya comin'? Huh?"

Maniac couldn't believe it. The ugly feelings of the other day showed nowhere on their excited faces.

"C'mon, Maniac. You *gotta!*"

And just like that, as he stared at them, the idea came, an idea as zany as they were. The words seemed to lift right off their faces, like sunburnt skin peeling. "Well, okay," he said, "on one condition."

"What's that?"

"If I can bring somebody with me."

"Sure! Bring *everybody!* We're gonna *party!*"

The librarian edged closer to the phone.

41

*T*he McNab boys didn't know whom they *did* expect Maniac to bring to the party, but one thing for sure — they did *not* expect him to come walking through the front door with a black kid.

And that was only half of it. From the way the kid swaggered in, from the candy bar that jutted like a chocolate stogie from the corner of his mouth, from the rip-stone-evil scowl on his face, the kid had to be none other than Mars Bar Thompson himself. If black meant bad, if black meant in-your-face nastiness, if black meant as far from white as you could get, then Mars Bar Thompson was the blackest of the black.

Here. In the middle of their living room. Stopping the party — the neighborhood kids, the Cobras, even George McNab — stopping them dead as traffic. Just walked in through the front door, the steel door. Breezed right on in. Past the bars. Standing there, I-own-this-jointing there, before they knew what was happening, before anyone could reach for anything.

Which, of course, is just what Maniac had had in

mind. Remembering how little Grayson had known about black people and black homes. Thinking of the McNabs' wrong-headed notions. Thinking of Mars Bar's knee-jerk reaction to anyone wearing a white skin. And thinking: *Naturally. What else would you expect? Whites never go inside blacks' homes. Much less inside their thoughts and feelings. And blacks are just as ignorant of whites. What white kid could hate blacks after spending five minutes in the Beales' house? And what black kid could hate whites after answering Mrs. Pickwell's dinner whistle?* But the East Enders stayed in the east and the West Enders stayed in the west, and the less they knew about each other, the more they invented.

It hadn't been easy: finding Mars Bar, taking all his lip about cheating on the race, taking some bumps, some shoves, Mars goading him to fight. But keeping his own cool, matching Mars Bar glare for glare, telling him he wasn't as bad as he thought he was. Really stoking him now, making him slam his candy bar to the ground. "No? You wanna tell me why I ain't so bad, fish? Go ahead, 'fore I waste ya." Chest to chest.

Keeping cool. Letting Mars do all the huffing. "Simple. You don't cross Hector. You stay over here, where it's safe. How bad would you be over there?" Stepping back then, folding his arms, smugging it up just enough, standing there in his white skin, gazing nonchalantly about, six-blocks-deep in the heart of the black side: "Guess that makes me badder than you."

*   *   *

They did not go straight to the McNabs'. First they went to the Pickwells'. Maniac wanted Mars Bar to see the best the West End had to offer.

The little Pickwells made as much fuss over Mars Bar as over Maniac. They believed, as did all little kids in the West End, that he carried a hundred Mars Bars with him at all times. Not surprisingly, Mrs. Pickwell never batted an eye when she saw who was coming to dinner.

It was quite a sight, all right — sixteen Pickwells plus Maniac, plus a down-and-out golf caddie — eighteen so-called white faces and Mars Bar Thompson. To his credit, Mars Bar didn't use the words "fish-belly" or "honky" once, though on one occasion he did bend the truth a mite. When a Pickwell kid asked him if it was true about the famous race in April, did Maniac really beat him going backward? — Mars Bar studied his fork for a minute and said, "Yeah, he went backward. But you got the story wrong. Wasn't me he beat. Was my brother, Milky Way." The little kids couldn't understand why the grownups laughed for five minutes after that.

As for Mars Bar himself, his expression never changed until the dinner was almost over, when the littlest non-baby Pickwell, Dolly, called him "Mr. Bar." And even then it wasn't so much a smile as a crack in the glare.

Even if Mars wasn't letting on, Maniac could tell he was pleased to learn his fame had spread to the West. When they left, half the Pickwell kids followed them, begging Mars to perform his legendary feat of stopping traffic.

"Don't," Maniac warned. "It might not work over here."

But the Pickwells persisted, and when they reached Marshall Street, Mars Bar commanded, "Stay here," and stepped into the traffic.

Not only did he shamble, jive, shuck, and hipdoodle at his own sweet pace, he did something he had never even done in the East End — he came to a complete and utter halt halfway across and let nothing but the evil in his eyes take care of the rest. He stood like that for one full minute. By the time he finally moved on to the far side, so the legend goes, twenty-three cars, several bicycles, and a bus were stacked to a dead stop in both directions. Maniac hurried across while the Pickwells stood at the curb, cheering and waving good-bye.

But no one was cheering now in Fort McNab. And Maniac knew that despite the swagger and the scowl and the chocolate stogie, Mars Bar Thompson was one uneasy dude.

42

George McNab was the first to speak up. He was stretched out on the only new piece of furniture in the house, a tilt-back lounge chair. Said McNab: "What's he doin' here?"

The awkward silence that followed was mercifully broken by Piper, tugging on Maniac's arm: "Where's my birthday present? Wha'd you get me?"

Maniac pulled the present from his pocket. Piper exclaimed: "A watch!"

"No," said Maniac. "A compass. It tells you which direction you're going."

"Like to the ocean?" asked Russell.

"The ocean, Mexico, anywhere in the world. Only one thing."

"What's that?"

Maniac took the compass from Piper's hand. "I'm keeping it till school's over. If you go every day — both of you — then you can have it back and sail around the world."

"On our raft!" Piper cheered.

"Is it a deal?"

Piper and Russell and Maniac did a three-way high-five. "It's a deal!"

George McNab pulled himself up from the easy chair and shuffled into the kitchen. He wore bare-backed slippers over bare feet. His white ankles were dirty. He took a beer can from the fridge and headed for the steps. "Let me know when it leaves," he said and went upstairs.

Maniac could feel the voltage that surged through Mars Bar and crackled black lightning from his eyes. Quickly he clapped his hands. "Hey — isn't this a party? Where're the games?"

So they played games. Silly games, whose main object seemed to be shrieking and screaming. Mars Bar allowed himself to be dragged into them, but his jaw was clenched and his eyes kept straying to the gaping hole in the ceiling — and to the Cobras, who were slouching against the walls and baseboards, sipping beers and watching his every move. None of them had spoken since Mars and Maniac walked in.

Of course, as far as the little kids were concerned, the highlight of the whole party was not the birthday boy, Piper McNab, but the McNab's new pillbox. They found every excuse to stay inside it. They fought over space at the narrow gunnery slots. When Mars Bar whispered to Maniac, "What *is* that?" Maniac said it was a bomb shelter.

Then Russell called: "Let's play Rebels! Whites in the pillbox, blacks outside."

A cheer went up, and a dozen kids stampeded into the pillbox. Their gabble circled the cinder-block walls and popped from the gunnery slots.

"I'm gonna be white!"

"*I'm* white!"

"Me, too!"

"Too many in here! We need more blacks!"

"Not me!"

"Not *me!*"

"We ain't got enough guns! Only the ones with the guns are in! The resta ya, get out! Yer black!"

"Gimme a gun!"

"I had it first!"

"C'mon, you meatballs — blacks is the best part. Ya get to charge."

"Yeah, we get to *lose!*"

"*Look* — you can use beer cans for grenades. You can lob *grenades!*"

"Then *you* do it!"

"Well, *some*body gotta be black, else we ain't playin'. I'm counting. Time I hit ten, I wanna see five-a ya *outta* here. One . . ."

Russell counted. No one came out, not at "nine," not at "ten," not after "ten." Maniac and Mars Bar stared in silence at the gunnery slots, where wide-open eyes began to appear, one pair atop another.

The three words that Mars Bar sneered, the joke that he spat out — "Yeah, bomb shelter" — did not even have the moment to themselves, for just then another word — "Geronimo!" — came plunging from the sky and landed with a floor-jarring, heart-stopping crash directly behind him. A Cobra had jumped from the hole, a fat, red-haired Cobra, who was now rolling on the floor and laughing so hard, as were all the Cobras, that his face matched the color of his hair. "Ya see him? Ya see him *jump?* I never seen . . . I never . . . See his face? Somebody check out his pants . . . check out his drawers . . . oh, man . . . oh . . . oh . . ."

Maniac had to wrap Mars Bar in a bear hug to keep him from charging the fat red roller. The laughter stopped as if cut by scissors. The Cobras were standing. John McNab sauntered forward. "You got a problem, sonny?"

"That wasn't funny, John," said Maniac. "He could've been hurt."

McNab kept his eyes on Mars Bar. "I ain't talkin' to you, Magee. I'm talking to sonny here. Don't you like our parties, sonny boy?"

Mars Bar strained against Maniac's arms. "You ain't got to worry about me comin' to no more your parties, fishbelly. And you ain't got to worry 'bout me invading this pisshole. Anybody come to a block away, they faint from the smell."

McNab advanced.

Maniac shouted: "John! You owe me one. I brought the boys back."

McNab took another step, then stayed. The Cobras stayed, and Maniac, clamping the struggling Mars Bar for dear life, lugged him down a gauntlet of seething eyes to the door and the street.

Mars Bar wrenched free and stomped on ahead. Maniac followed. It was almost dark. High above, the streetlights were buzzing on, one by one.

After several blocks, Mars Bar wheeled. "You suckered me. You soften me up with them Pick-peoples, then bring me here. Wha'd you think? I was gonna *cry?* Okay, I come over. I did it. It's done. And don't you be comin' 'round no more, ya hear me, fish? 'Cause you ain't only seen me *half* bad yet."

He turned and headed due east. Maniac walked another way.

It was a good question. What *had* he thought? What had he expected? A miracle? Well, come to think of it, maybe one had happened. While he was looking for one miracle, maybe another had snuck up on him. It happened as he was clamping and lugging Mars Bar down the gauntlet of Cobras, trying to keep him alive — and what was Mars Bar doing? Fighting *him,* Maniac, straining to get loose and bust some Cobras. Out-numbered, out-weighed, but not out-hearted. That's when Maniac felt it — pride, for this East End warrior whom Maniac could feel trembling in his arms, scared as any normal kid would be, but not showing it to them. Yeah, you're bad all right, Mars Bar. You're more than bad. You're good.

Maniac stopped. He had been walking in circles. It was dark. He turned one way, then another, for the briefest moment thinking to go home. Thinking, it's time to go home now. Then remembering that once again he had no home to go to.

43

*H*e slept in the park that night, and for the next dozen or so. Sometimes in the buffalo shed; other times the band shell benches or the pavilion. The nights were warm now. June was on the way.

He ate when and where he could. For apples and carrots and day-old hamburger buns, you couldn't beat the deer and buffalo pens. A new Acme had opened, and the bakery section always had a tray of free samples sitting on the counter.

And then there were always the Pickwells. It may have been an illusion, but it seemed that the hungrier he got, the farther Mrs. Pickwell's whistle traveled. Some dinnertimes, there was hardly a spot in town from which he could not hear it.

He read in the library. He joined pickup games in the park — baseball, basketball. School was letting out. There were more kids.

Mornings were the best. He would rise with the sun's color, before the sun itself, before the bison, and set out. He came to think of these appleskin hours as his special time with the town. There was not a street or alleyway or house or store, not even a garage, that he did not recognize. His footsteps fell everywhere but on the bridge over the Schuylkill, his eyes everywhere but on the P & W trolley trestle.

And the people — most of them he did not know by name or face, yet they revealed themselves to him even as they slept. He knew them by their windows and cars and porches and toys they left outside. But most of all, he knew them by their backyards. Flowers, weeds, junk, pet houses, tree houses, vegetable gardens, rubber tires, grass ranging from desert-sparse to shaggy to trim as a marine's haircut — the backyards were as different, as individual as faces.

East End and West End, black and white would begin only when the alarm clocks rang. For now, before sunrise, there were no divisions, no barriers. There were only the people, the families, the town. His town. As much his town as anyone's.

He knew he could be sleeping right then in the Beales' house, or the Pickwells', or even the McNabs'. But beyond that, for a few enchanted moments each newborn morning, he believed there was not a single home in Two Mills, not a single one, that would not happily welcome him to enter and to go upstairs and curl up between its sleepers. Maybe that's why he left his band shell bench late one night in mid-June and went to someone's backyard on Hamilton Street, someone whose leaf lettuce he had watched growing, and quietly opened the gate and closed it behind him and laid himself down on a white wicker loveseat on the back porch.

From then on, he slept in a different backyard or back porch every night. Once, finding the back door unlocked, he slept in a kitchen.

44

*O*ne morning in early July, cruising down the appleskin hour, Maniac thought he heard footsteps other than his own. He stopped. Only the vast quietness responded.

It happened a few more times. Must be his own footfalls echoing down the row house canyons.

Two days later, passing an alley, he thought something moved at the other end. And once, turning onto a broad street, he had the feeling, more sense than sight, that something had just flashed around a corner two blocks away.

When these odd sensations continued for another morning or two, Maniac knew he was not alone.

So he was not totally surprised when, a few mornings later, he turned a corner and ran smack into another early-hour cruiser. No, it wasn't the *what* that surprised him, it was the *who:* Mars Bar Thompson.

They quickly bounced off each other and went their separate ways. Neither paused. Neither said a word.

This was the first in a series of apparently random mergings. Intersections, alleyways — one never knew when he would come upon the other. Sometimes they found themselves running the same route, only a block apart. On one occasion, they trotted down the same street at the same time in the same direction, but on opposite sides of the street.

And then one day, as it happened, they each turned a particular corner at the same moment and headed off in the same direction, side by side. Still neither spoke. Not even their eyes met. They jogged silently for a block, then veered apart.

The next time they dovetailed, they stayed that way for two blocks, then three blocks, and so on. No words, no looks, just the rhythmic slapping of their sneaker soles upon the sidewalk and the pulsing duet of their breathings. Stride for stride, shoulder to shoulder, breath for breath, till they were matching on all points, a harnessed pair, two runners become one.

Morning after morning it happened this way — the two of them dovetailing at an intersection, and, without the slightest hitch in stride, cruising off together. Though each face showed no awareness of the other, they were in fact minutely sensitive to each other. If Mars Bar cranked up the pace just a notch, Maniac would pick it up within a stride; if Maniac inched ahead, Mars Bar was there. If one veered to the left or right, the other followed like a shadow. One day one was the leader, the next day the other.

One day Mars Bar would lead Maniac down the

river, down the tracks, past the railroad gondolas, each with its mountain of coal, to the rolling mill at the steel plant where his father worked. Another day, Maniac would head for the townships to the north and west, the farmlands of the county, where dew sparkled on spider webs, and nature was doing such fresh and wonderful things that you could almost hear the long, neat congregations of corn clapping "A-men" and "A-*men!*"

When the workingpeople began leaving their houses, the daybreak boys diverged, Mars Bar to the East End, Maniac to wherever.

A week passed. A second week. Morning after morning. Stride for stride, breath by breath. Never a word, never a glance. Each believing the other simply happened to be going where he was going.

They were cruising Main Street one morning, passing the Grand movie theater, when Piper McNab came screaming down the middle of the empty street. He was wild-eyed and crying and soaking wet. His feet were slathered in coal-black mud. He shrieked and babbled at them, but he made no sense, so they just followed as he raced frantically back up the street. As they ran, the belchlike toot of a whistle grew louder and louder.

He led them to the corner of Main and Swede, to where the platform of the P & W trolley terminal hung high above the sidewalk. He burst into the terminal building and up the steps. In a moment Maniac and Mars Bar were on the platform, gasping and following Piper's pointing finger down the tracks. What they saw pulled the fragments of Piper's babble together.

The boys had been playing Bombs Away. Piper's part was to sail the raft down the river. Russell's part was to wait on the trolley trestle that spanned the river, and when Piper passed underneath, bomb away from a bucketful of rocks.

Everything went as planned — unless you count Russell's failing to sink the raft, and Piper's practically drowning trying to beach it — until Piper returned to the terminal to find Russell still out on the trestle. Apparently, without the target below to focus on, Russell had suddenly discovered how high he was. One false step, and he could slip right between the ties to the river.

And that's where Russell was now, out on the middle of the trestle, high over the water, frozen in terror, not even a railing to cling to, responding neither to Piper's cries nor to the red-and-yellow P & W trolley, which also occupied the trestle, idling and tooting about twenty feet away.

Piper pulled at Maniac. "Save him! Save him!"

Mars Bar stared with growing astonishment at Maniac, whose wide, unblinking eyes were fixed on the trestle, yet somehow did not seem to register what was there. Nor did he seem to hear Piper pleading. With the drenched, mud-footed kid clawing at him, he turned without a word, without a gesture, and left the platform and went downstairs. Shortly he appeared on the sidewalk below. He crossed Main and continued walking slowly up Swede, Piper screaming after him from the end of the platform.

45

"*M*agee! . . . Magee! . . ."

Maniac's first groggled thought was that it was the buffalo calling to him. Then he thought, *It's the Superintendent. He's discovered me, and he's come to kick me out.*

He propped himself on his elbow, swatted a straw from his ear, and gave a better listen.

"Magee! . . . *Magee!*"

Mars Bar.

It was the second night following the morning at the trestle. Maniac had been asleep in the buffalo lean-to.

He stood.

"Magee!"

"Where are you?"

"Here. Over *here.*"

He headed toward the voice over the hoof-chopped earth. The moon was full. He could see Mars Bar's dark form against the fence. Then he could see his eyes.

"What're you doing here?"

"I been lookin' for ya. I heard you hung out here."

"Where did you hear that?"

"Amanda Beale. You really sleep here, man?"

"What do you want?"

"Where's the buffaloes? I can't see 'em."

"They're sleeping. Like every other person that's got sense. What're you doing out here at this time of night?"

"I snuck out. I'm not there when they wake up, they'll figure I'm out running, like usual. Ain't you afraid in there?"

"No."

Both fell silent. Crickettalk and fireflies held the night.

"Magee?"

"Yeah?"

"I got to ask you something."

"Go ahead."

"Why'd you . . . why didn't you go after the kid? Why'd you go away?"

Maniac didn't answer.

"Listen, man, I know you wasn't scared. I know it. So I had to come ask ya."

Maniac's voice came faintly, "Is he okay?"

"I asked you first."

Maniac drew a long breath. "You want to come in?"

Mars Bar laughed. "You kidding? Ain't no buffalo gonna eat this dude."

"They don't eat people."

"You come out here, man."

Maniac climbed the fence. He started to walk. Mars

Bar walked with him. Maniac told him the story of his parents' death. He told about his problem with the trestle, how he had learned to avoid it. "And then, all of a sudden, there I was, on the platform, looking out at it, closer to it than I ever was before, up on the same level. I always saw it from below before. Now I was up there, too, where they were, looking down, and it was more real than ever. The nightmare was worse than ever. I saw the trolley coming . . . I saw it . . . f-falling . . . them . . . them . . ."

They walked in silence past the silo-shaped cage of the broken-winged golden eagle.

Mars Bar swallowed hard. His voice was hoarse. "I knew you wasn't scared."

Maniac sniffed. "I don't remember much. Next thing I knew, I was somewhere on Swede Street."

"Somebody come down the East End like you did, all by hisself, a fishbelly, get all up in my face" — he rippled a stick along the deer-pen fence — "I *knew* scared wasn't it."

"So," said Maniac, "what happened?"

Mars Bar laughed, wagged his head. "Happened? Man, I *still* don't believe it." He rippled the fence. "That little honky, he looks at me all his crybaby face and says okay, can *I* go out and get his brother? I look around, like, is somebody else here? I says to him, 'Who you talkin' to? Me?' I'm just pullin' his chain, only he don't know it. 'Cause I'm ticked a little, y'know, 'cause there he was hollerin' for you up the street, and there I am standing right alongside the damn stupid white potata, understand what I'm sayin'?"

Maniac nodded, and out of the darkness came the strangest sound — a kind of amplified gulp.

Mars Bar jumped. "What's that?"

"Emu," said Maniac. "There."

Behind the nearest fence loomed a tall, thin neck topped by a small head. "E-*what?*"

"E-*mu*. Second-largest bird in the world, after the ostrich. They're from Australia."

"I don't remember studyin' about no emu. You buddies with all these dudes?"

"No, just the buffalo. So, go ahead, what happened?"

"What happened" — Mars Bar snorted — "what happened was, I went out and rescued the dumb fish. Like to get myself kilt."

Maniac touched Mars Bar's arm. "He's okay?"

Mars Bar snickered. "Yeah, he's okay, but that ain't the main part. The main part is, how he was all grabbin' on to me comin' off them tracks. Shakin'. Shiverin'. Huggin'. Like he wanted to climb inside me. I was afraid" — he shook his head, giggled — "afraid the fishbelly was gonna kiss me."

They laughed. Maniac tried to picture it, the two of them, making their way across the trestle, tie by tie, arms wrapped around each other.

"And even *that* ain't the mainest part," said Mars Bar, his voice rising in wonder. "Even when we got off, the midget wouldn't let me go. 'We're off it,' I says to him. 'You're rescued.' But all he does is grab me harder, like he's a octopus or somethin'. Off the platform, down the steps, out to the street — he's still doin' it. I couldn't pry him off nohow."

"So," said Maniac, "what *did* you do?"

"Wha'd I *do?* I took him home."

Maniac stopped dead. *"What?"*

Mars Bar shrugged. "I figured, let my mom pry him off me. 'Course, the other one had to come too. But I made him leave them muddy sneakers outside." He put his nose to a fence. "What's in there? I don't see nothin'."

"Prairie Dog Town. They're underground. So, what then?"

"So, my mother took over. She pried the one off me, and soon's she does, he jumps right onto her, like a octopus. I go to pull him off and she gets all mad at *me* and says let him go, let him go. She gets the wet one dried off. Takes off his clothes and puts my old stuff on him. Stuff she been savin' case I get a little brother someday. But I won't, 'cause my mom can't have no babies no more. And I ain't even come to the craziest part yet."

"What's that?"

"They didn't wanna go home. They stayed all day. My mother babyin' 'em, feedin' 'em. I tell her not to, she swats me away. Sometimes my mom ain't got no sense. She makes me play games with them. Monopoly and stuff. Finally my father drives them home. It's after dark. They're getting out the car, and know what they say to me — I'm in the car too — " He wagged his head. "They ask me to come in and play that game-a theirs. Rebels. They, like, beg me. They say, 'Come on — *pleeeeese* — if you *play* with us, we'll let you be *white*.' You *believe* that?"

Maniac chuckled. "I believe it."

They walked on.

"Magee?"

"Yeah?"

"I had to ask you something. Now I gotta tell you something."

"What's that?"

"You smell like a buffalo."

Ears of a hundred different shapes prickled at the long, loud laughter of the boys.

"Magee?" Mars Bar said, after a spell.

"Yeah?"

"My mother wants to ask you something, too."

"Your mother?"

"Yeah. Like I told her about you, y'know. Actually, she already heard about you."

"So?"

"She wants to know, like, uh, why don't you come to our house?"

Maniac turned, stared directly at Mars Bar. Mars Bar looked away. He said nothing more.

They walked on, silent among the crickets and fireflies.

Having made a full circle of the zoo, they were back at the pen of the American bison. Maniac said, "I can't."

"Why not?" said Mars Bar. "My house not good enough? My mother?"

Maniac struggled for words. "I didn't say I didn't want to. It's just . . . I don't know . . . things happen . . . I can't . . ."

"Look, man," Mars Bar snapped, "ain't nobody

sayin' come *live* with us. All we sayin'—all *she* sayin'—is, you wanna come for a little, you know, visit? You *want* to? Well, come on, you can. That's all. Don't go makin' no big thing, man. Ain't no big thing."

Maniac shuddered. He turned his eyes to the sky, beyond the flickering fireflies to the stars. If there were answers, they were as far away as the constellations. "I gotta go," he said, and before Mars Bar could react, he was over the fence and hurrying for the lean-to.

46

*T*he teeth of the buffalo clamped firmly upon his ear and lifted his head up from the straw, up from sleep.

Mars Bar was right! They DO eat people!

The buffalo did more than bring great pain to his ear. It spoke to him.

"Ain't you nice . . . ain't you nice . . ."

But the voice of the buffalo was the voice of Amanda Beale, and its teeth were her fingers pulling and wrenching his poor ear till he was sitting upright.

"See *that*," she snapped, and scrambled his brains with a smack to the head. He'd rather she pulled his ear. "There you go, making me say ain't. I *have not* said that word all year long, and now you go making me *soooo* mad." She snatched a handful of straw and flung it at him.

"I'm *sorry*," he said. He wondered if he would have better luck sleeping in the emu pen. "Can I ask a question?"

"Make it quick," she growled.

"Except for making you say ain't, what is it I'm saying I'm sorry for?"

"What?" she screeched. She was standing above him, hands on hips. He didn't need the light of day to feel the look on her face. "You're *sorry* for a whole mess of things, boy. You're *sorry* because you didn't accept Snickers's invitation to his house. And you're *sorry* because he came throwing a ball up against my bedroom window and waking me up and telling me I had to get up *out* of my bed and sneak *out* of my house in the *middle* of the night and come *out* here and do something about all *this*. That is why you are *sorry,* boy."

Maniac yawned. "Snickers?"

"That's what I'm changing his name to. How *bad* can you act if everybody's calling you" — she said it loud —"Snickers?"

A voice came rasping from the fence. "Shut up, girl."

Maniac howled with laughter. It struck him that it had been a long time since he had reared back like this, so he just let the laughter carry on as long as it wanted.

When he finally settled down, Amanda said, "Okay, let's go."

"Huh?" said Maniac.

"Let's go."

"Where?"

"Home."

"Whose?"

"Mine. Yours. Ours. Come on, I'm sleepy."

Oh, no. Maniac opened his mouth to speak, to pro-
test, to explain — but there was too much. A hundred
nights would not be long enough to explain, to make
her understand. So he simply said, "I can't," and lay
back down.

In an instant he was bolt upright again, yanked by
a hand he couldn't believe belonged to a girl. "Don't
tell me *can't.* I didn't come all the way out here in my
nightshirt and my slippers and climb that fence and
almost kill myself so I could hear you tell me *can't!*"
She was yelling. Several pens away, Prairie Dog Town
stirred. Heads popped into the moonlight. "You got
it all wrong, buster. You ain't got — ouuu, *see*" — she
kicked him —"you *do not* have a choice. I am not
asking you. I'm *telling* you. You are coming home
with me, and you are going to sleep in *my* room, which
is going to be *your* room — and I don't care if you
sleep on the floor or the windowsill or what — but
you are going to sleep *there* and not *here.* And you are
going to sleep there tonight and *tomorrow* night and
the night after *that* and the night after *that* and *every*
night, except maybe once in a while if you decide to
sleep over at Snickers's house, *if* he ever asks you
again. *This* is *not* your *home!* Now *move!*"

She jerked him to his feet. Applause and a brief
whistle came from the fence.

Amanda led him by the hand across the muddy,
lumpy earth. "Boost me," she commanded at the
fence. He boosted her. Mars Bar helped her down
from the other side. Maniac hesitated, then climbed
over himself.

They walked through the zoo and down the boulevard, the three of them, Amanda and Mars Bar/Snickers and Maniac, Amanda grumbling all the way: ". . . You're more trouble *outside* the house than *in* it . . . Now I'm gonna have to throw these slippers away. There's probably buffalo poop all over them . . . And you better *not* come within ten feet of me, boy, till you get a *bath* . . ."

Maniac said nothing. He was quite content to let Amanda do the talking, for he knew that behind her grumbling was all that he had ever wanted. He knew that finally, truly, at long last, someone was calling him home.